THE CURSE OF LEMNOS

THEY STEPPED OUTSIDE, leaving behind them the greed, lying and horror inside the building. Milliya took his hand. It was probably dusk—who could tell? On Terra there was never much daylight. Even during the day, the dim lights of the city would be left on, to flicker through the permanent Terran smog.

Except that, astonishingly, it wasn't dark. Hand in hand, they stared in amazement. Westwards from the city, the impenetrable wall of smog had cleared, as though someone had battered a hole in it, and Helios sat, huge and round, on the distant horizon. When it sank below it, there would definitely be darkness.

Burk and Milliya turned to each other, and as they did so the star trembled, slipped, and flashed its light one last time across everything, like a sudden, blinding reflection off metal; or the signal of the coming end of a planet.

THE CURSE OF LEMNOS

FRANCIS JARMAN

WILDSIDE PRESS

"A plague o' both your houses"

—William Shakespeare, *Romeo and Juliet*

Published by Wildside Press LLC.
www.wildsidepress.com

PROLOGUE

REPORT FROM LEMNOS SUBMITTED BY GUARDIAN GRADE IV (PROVISIONAL) SOUSANNA ALPHEIOS (CRIME AND SECURITY)

Document Status: Top Secret
Security Clearance: Grades IV-V only
Code: Z-LE-06-319-4*

Respectful greetings! The situation on Lemnos has taken an unpredicted turn. Unfortunately the problem can no longer be resolved here on the planet, and has developed a certain political dimension. It is therefore my belief that firm measures are now called for, on Terra, which take the political sensitivity of the matter into account. It can no longer be dealt with by my own Department of Crime and Security as a purely legal/criminal issue.

I was initially detailed to travel to Lemnos on the people transporter *Starstretcher* to investigate upon arrival the illegal destruction by the Lemnian settlers of the unique and valuable indigenous life form known as *sqot* (Intellreport Z-LE-06-316-3*). *Sqot* is the most advanced alien life form so far discovered within the Terran Empire, and its eradication would be a cause of embarassment to the Imperial Government.

As a result of intelligence received only after my embarkation (Intellreport H-TE-06-7144920-3*), I was assigned a second task: to apprehend and neutralize the **AdPop (Lower Executive Level) John Burk**, who was employed on a temporary basis in the Social and Recreational Department of the *Starstretcher*. According to this information Burk had been recruited by elements close to the Imperial Advisory Council, which was working not for the first time at cross purposes to the Imperial Government. He was to travel unobtrusively to Lemnos, collect specially prepared documentation "proving" Government responsibility for the destruction of *sqot*, and return equally unobtrusively to Terra with this potentially explosive material as evidence and himself as a witness.

It was necessary for me to launch an on-board enquiry into supposed pedophile activities of AdPop Burk, enabling him to be detained on the *Starstretcher*, refused disembarkation on Lemnos, and returned safely to Terra. Here he could be interrogated systematically regarding his involvement in the activities of the Imperial Advisory Council; the fabricated charges against him could be quietly dropped, as and when convenient, in return for his cooperation.

The on-board enquiry was complicated by the presence of **Guardian Grade III (Senior Level) Rebek'a Lascaris (Ideology)**, known to have influential friends on the Imperial Advisory Council. AdPop Burk may have been honeytrapped and recruited by Guardian Rebek'a's former lover **Guardian Grade I (Intermediate Level) Milliya Jahangiri (Crime and Security)**. Unknown to me, Guardian Milliya had smuggled herself onto the *Starstretcher* in the guise of "Guardian Grade I (Intermediate Level) Jo-anna Corticelli (Crime and Security)", whom Guardian Milliya or her accomplices had previously murdered and robbed of her identity.

The third member of the enquiry, **Guardian Grade III Adriyan (Social and Recreational)** committed suicide under suspicious circumstances, and there was apparently a falling-out among the conspirators. Guardian Rebek'a was tasered unconscious, and Adpop Burk and Guardian Milliya disembarked at the Gate of Lemnos under false identities. What their intentions at that point were remains unclear.

On the return flight Guardian Rebek'a, having recovered consciousness, demanded that the Commander of the *Starstretcher*, **Guardian Grade IV Mykel Angelos**, change course and return to Lemnos. The Commander rightly refused. Guardian Rebek'a then jumped ship, taking advantage of an in-flight docking with a Lemnos-bound freighter that wished to transfer a seriously ill crew-member to the better medical facilities of the *Starstretcher* (Intellreport SF-SR-06-31-3* from Guardian Mykel, who has also filed a Form 85a Complaint about Guardian Rebek'a's behavior).

Despite having no valid documentation, Guardian Rebek'a bullied her way through security, identity and customs checks at the Gate of Lemnos [Recommendation: procedures and personnel at the Gate should be overhauled as a matter of urgency, since within no more than a few days three incoming persons with false or non-existent ID were permitted to disembark]. She then liaised with her friends in the Planetary Governorate and among the settlers, and tracked her quarry down at a location in the remote and barren area known as the Other Side. My own arrival there (I was able to locate the two fugitives when Guardian Milliya switched on her personal communicator) may have been just in time to prevent her from killing them.

In the course of the stand-off with Guardian Rebek'a, who threatened me with her taser, I was forced to allow the fugitives to escape, but I extracted a solemn promise from Guardian Milliya that she and AdPop Burk would present themselves to Crime and Security in the near future to answer the charges against them. (That should not be a problem for AdPop Burk, who has not to my knowledge committed any serious offence and who is a trivial rather than a dangerous person; also, he has nowhere else to go. But Guardian Milliya will face a possible charge of murder, in the case of Guardian Jo-anna, and of grievous bodily harm, in the case of Guardian Rebek'a, should the letter choose to testify against her—there are emotional complications here.)

I had no warrant to arrest Guardian Rebek'a, and she still outranked me at that time. I could not win her cooperation in my enquiries, or that of the Security Guardians from Lemnos City, and I was therefore unable to detain Guardian Rebek'a's dubious "friends" at the location, whom I strongly suspected of being involved in criminal or even terroristic activities. Soil samples at the site were taken, but have since gone astray somewhere in the Planetary Governorate offices, where I was given no support or encouragement in my investigation, even when I was advanced provisionally to Guardian Grade IV rank [Recommendation: new soil samples should be taken by trusted personnel as soon as possible. I have submitted the detailed coordinates of the location in a separate message].

The two fugitives have disappeared. It is unlikely that they have chosen to remain on Lemnos, where they are officially outlaws, are seen as traitors by the settlers, and have broken away from their Imperial Advisory Council support network. It is more likely that they are already en route back to Terra, traveling on either the *Starspringer*, which left the Gate yesterday, or on a freighter, and under new false identities. This deception can only have been organized for them by dissident elements ("Ciaranite" anarchists?) within the ranks of the Guardians. However, it should not be too difficult to crack these false identities and apprehend Guardian Milliya and AdPop Burk when they attempt to disembark.

Both Guardian Rebek'a and I will be returning to Terra on the people transporter *Starsearcher*, embarking tomorrow. Should I happen to discover the fugitives on board the transporter, which is admittedly unlikely, I shall detain them and (in consultation with the Commander of the vessel) have them placed in separate holding cells, but I shall not undertake any systematic interrogation.

My attempts to have Guardian Rebek'a placed in detention here on Lemnos, pending investigation of the Form 85A Complaint against her, have been unsuccessful. She has obtained an Imperial Rescript, signed by the Secretary to the Imperial Advisory Council, **His Excellency Count Stelios Dagon**, requiring her to return at once to Terra and place herself at the disposal of the authorities but granting her full immunity from arrest or interrogation for the interim period [Recommendation 1: that Guardian Rebek'a be detained immediately upon arrival by a senior Guardian from Crime and Security, before she can be spirited away by agents of the Imperial Advisory Council or by Guardians from her own Department of Ideology; Recommendation 2: that the process by which the Imperial Rescript came to be issued be most carefully scrutinized—is His Imperial Majesty aware of what is being authorized in His name?].

For understandable reasons, it is unlikely that Guardian Rebek'a and I will be socializing with each other very much during the journey.

No witnesses were present, for security reasons, but the date and full details of the name and rank of the author are encoded in the protocol. The document is authenticated to Security Level 5 by my electronic voiceprint.

CHAPTER ONE

AN UNCOMFORTABLE PLACE TO
BE (BUT THERE ARE WORSE)

Burk and Milliya were arrested the moment they dis-embarked. And none too gently.

"Hello 'Miley'. Hello 'Mytt'. Or is it 'Markko Mann' and 'Guardian Jo-anna'? Whoever you are, welcome back to Terra."

Then a gloved fist had smacked into Burk's face, and he was dragged away. Slipping into semi-consciousness, he didn't see what happened to Milliya, though she told him later that she'd been knocked and kicked about, screamed at ("You bitch! Fucking *an AdPop*!") and strip-searched. This was roughly the same treatment that Burk was given—and which Milliya had warned him to ex-pect—except that with him they had really gone to town (and they had shouted "Fucking *a Guardian*!").

Milliya would have said, "Why shouldn't they be angry?" After all, he wasn't a Guardian like Milliya; he was only an AdPop, and he was a man. In the Guardian team that battered him there was only one male, and he was the sensitive one: he pulled his punches, and looked away awkwardly when the Grade II Guardian in com-mand, Pigface (she hadn't bothered to introduce herself), probed his nether regions with unnecessary vigor.

"Ow! If you're looking for *sqot*, you won't find any *up there*."

That had been a mistake. Pigface had redoubled her efforts, rather painfully, and when they indeed found nothing Burk was soon being bounced off the walls and against the sharp edges of furniture. Later, when he told Milliya about it, and suggested that he might not be able to sit in comfort without a cushion, instead of offering him one, or any sympathy, she had merely shrugged.

"Why should she be gentle? It's not part of the training. Don't make such a fuss! What a baby you are! You're still in one piece, aren't you? And what did you call her? Pigface? That's not very nice. I might even know her. She could have done basic training with me."

It was a good sign, she said, that they hadn't been put in separate holding cells and were being allowed to talk to each other. That showed that (quite rightly) no-one suspected them of anything really serious, and that they knew that she and Burk had been duped by that wicked Guardian Rebek'a and her vicious friends. It was good that they were being held in protective custody. Their testimony would be so important in bringing those wicked people to justice!

While she was saying this, she looked sharply at Burk to gain his attention and then twitched her left eyelid. It was less than even a wink, and it was one of the micro-signals that they had agreed upon while they were on the *Starspringer*: if they were arrested—no, *when* they were arrested—they might be held together deliberately in order to monitor their conversation with recording devices. When that happened, they must know what to feed their eavesdropping friends. She was reminding him to keep to their agreed text.

Technically, they hadn't been arrested, only detained, which was easy to do under the Terran Security Laws. Proper arrest, on the other hand, meant that you had to be charged, or taken before a judge. They had to justify what they were doing, and there was a lot of paperwork, and if they made a mistake it might come back and bite them, so formal arrest had gone out of fashion long ago. Who needed the extra work? Who wanted to mess up their career? Detention was much, much easier.

It was so obvious that neither of them actually needed to say it: the Guardians weren't sure what to do with them yet. They were in the hands of Crime and Security, not the dreaded Ideology Section. Perhaps their captors were waiting for the return of Guardian Sousanna?

There was also the little matter of the recordings that Milliya had made on Lemnos, and the soil samples that she had taken. Milliya had done an initial scan of the samples, and said, "Interesting…but you wouldn't understand it, Burk." She had hidden everything very cleverly on board the *Starspringer*, and with even greater cunning she had arranged for it to be unloaded to a safe destination on Terra. Burk was not told where, or how.

He was used to not being told things.

"You don't need to know the details," she had said. "If they use truth drugs or torture on me, I might be able to trick them for a while—I don't know, but I've got the training at least. You would buckle straight away. So it's better for you not to know too much."

The communicator and the soil samples were their life insurance policy, and in three directions—because they were trapped between three powerful, dangerous and unfriendly organizations.

The Government wanted to know what was happening on Lemnos. Who was stripping *sqot* from the planet's surface? And who were the Outsiders, who had been murdering and mutilating their way across the interplanetary transportation lanes? The recordings on Milliya's communicator would answer those questions, but after that? The Government apparently had its own agenda regarding *sqot*, which was to factory-farm it as an addictive drug. So much for altruism! Burk and Milliya already knew too much, and could become an embarrassment. They needed to keep themselves alive, and their evidence hidden, until there was a public hearing or a judicial enquiry, after which they would be too famous to be "disappeared."

Guardian Rebek'a and her friends on the Imperial Advisory Council had created the *sqot* scandal in order to bring down the Government. And the Outsiders were more than just a smokescreen. They were doing something very sinister on Lemnos, and the soil samples that Milliya had taken would provide an answer. But if Burk and Milliya could be removed from the picture and the material evidence disposed of, then the fake recordings they had been given by Rebek'a's settler friend Jonn could be brought into play, and the Government could still be toppled.

The Ciaranites were helping Burk and Milliya, but why? They were terrorists, everyone knew that. They hated the Government. They hated the Emperor. Did they hate Guardian Rebek'a and the Outsiders even more? Were they trying to cause a complete melt-down, the collapse of all the structures of law and govenment, in order to plunge the universe into anarchy? They were using

Burk and Milliya, but not out of kindness. They would drop them the moment that they ceased to be useful.

The door to the holding cell slid open and the Guardian that Milliya had called Pigface marched in with a tray of food. Well, you wouldn't really call it food—it was an assortment of nutrition bars and packets of concentrate, dull rations of the DELICIO brand, which, as Burk immediately noticed, were intended exclusively for AdPop consumption. So not the best quality. This was standard fare for him, but as a Guardian Milliya had normally eaten better than this.

In fact, *both* of them had eaten better than this on Lemnos. Burk sighed nostalgically as he remembered the feasts served up on Jonn's estate: the fresh bread, the exquisitely cooked Lemnian vegetables, the honey-glazed meat dripping with gravy, the quivering blancmanges and jellies, the ripe bananas, the crisp tartlets filled with Goro-nut paste…

If they needed any confirmation that the Guardians had been spying on them, Pigface's pronounced surliness towards Burk (even more than an AdPop lowlife would normally have merited) and the "Fuck you!" that she silently mouthed in his direction could be so interpreted.

Milliya smiled at her sweetly.

"Thank you for your kindness, Guardian."

Pigface grunted at her noncommittedly, added "Drink comes later" as an afterthought, glared once again at Burk, and left.

Had the rations been doctored with tranquillizer, or a truth drug? No, that would have been far too much work. And it would have been more suspicious if they'd served them something fresh.

That was because fresh food was rare on Terra. Centuries ago, most of the farming land had been polluted and violated way beyond the help of even the most high-powered fertilizers. Synthetic foods had become the norm, though it was known that recycled human organic material played a distinct role in their production. This was waste matter, left over after all re-usable parts and organs had been harvested.

The whole subject was embarrassing, and taboo. No-one talked about it. No-one even liked to think about it. Typically, it had been the first issue that Ciaran Burke had raised, at the beginning of what turned into a massive terrorist movement. Dr. Ciaran himself came to a sticky and painful end, and the Ciaranite uprising was drowned in blood. (Was blood recycled too? Burk wasn't sure. Milliya might know.)

They ate quickly. There was no reason to linger over the "food," most of which tasted of nothing in particular. With the rations for UsePops and Guardians they made more of an effort to make the stuff taste reasonable.

They looked around the cell. What should they do now? Milliya clearly had something in mind. She pulled Burk towards her, and began to kiss him. After all, they might soon be separated and not see each other for a long time. She took his hand and placed it between her legs, then nicked her head in the direction of the plain single bed that filled one corner of the cell. Burk felt her heat. She wanted much more than a cuddle!

It was normal for women to initiate sex, and there was nothing wrong with that, but Burk wasn't completely happy. Were they perhaps being filmed as well as sound-recorded? He wasn't an exhibitionist. There wasn't even a sheet or blanket that they could use as a covering.

Burk imagined how indignant the watching Guardians might already be, seeing their colleague touching and caressing him. How much more enraged they would be if they had to watch her "taken" by a filthy AdPop, especially if Milliya allowed him to mount her from above or from behind instead of their adopting the recommended position for sex, in which the woman was always on top and always in command... What a delightful thought!

Would the Guardians rush into the cell and beat him to a pulp? Would he be charged with a gross sexual misdemeanor? Burk was never to know, because once again the door slid open and a group of Guardians entered, but this time more sedately, and not in a manner that suggested moral outrage or vengeful spite.

There were three of them. One was the comparatively gentle male Guardian who had participated in the beating that Burk had been given (Burk thought of him as "Mr. Sensitive," though all things are relative); the other two were female Guardians whom he had never seen before, one of them with the double red shoulder slash that marked her as a non-commissioned officer, a Grade II.

Although he was outranked, and distinctly nervous, it was the man who spoke first.

"These Guardian colleagues have come to interview you. I'll leave you in their capable hands."

Neither of the women spoke until he had left the room. Then the Grade II turned to her colleague and said, "Take a good look at this one. Treacherous *filth*. Its name is Milliya Jahangiri. That is what a traitor looks like."

Milliya smiled.

"Hello, Julieta. Always the drama queen! So nice to see you again. Won't you introduce me to our pretty colleague? Is she a good fuck?"

Guardian Julieta stiffened, and went bright red. She herself was athletically built, slim and quite good-looking, in what Burk always thought of as the "gym instructor style". Her junior colleague, however, was an absolute stunner, with a porcelain complexion, blonde curls, a pretty snub-nose and bee-stung lips. She looked more like an expensive item from a pleasure android catalog than a human being. (Androids were of course not allowed into the ranks of the Guardians, whatever the Guardians' sometimes dehumanized, thuggish behavior might lead you to think.)

"She is not *your* colleague. You lost the right to call her that when you ratted on us."

"Oh, and when would that be? When I *started* shagging your boss, or when I *stopped*? Rebek'a's always had a rapid turnover in girlfriends—you don't need to take it personally."

Guardian Julieta put a finger to her lips.

"Shhh!"

"Yes, yes: you don't want to discuss sensitive matters, do you? After all, who knows who might be listening? You'd prefer to take us with you, I'm sure, back to Ideology and down to the cellars, for some knockabout fun. But someone here in a fancy uniform seems to have said 'no'."

"Don't be stupid!"

So far Burk had felt slightly left out of this conversation, though admiring the charms of Guardian Julieta's young colleague (it was enough to make you apply for Guardian training) he was not exactly bored. Now Milliya turned towards him.

"*Darling*, may I introduce you to Guardian Julieta, from the Ideology Section—you remember, the mind police and torturers? The nasty mob? I don't know the other one. She doesn't look right for the part."

"My name is Jeena."

Miss Bee-sting had an improbably husky, masculine-sounding voice, which if anything made her more rather than less attractive. And she tossed her curls most charmingly. Guardian Julieta flashed an unpleasant look at her.

"Just keep quiet."

"Ah, yes, that's how trainees were treated in my day, too. Is she permanently attached to you, for *intensive training*, or could we borrow her for an afternoon? It's boring in here, and I don't think we'll be going anywhere else very soon. Certainly not in the direction of *your* department."

"Wait and see, Milliya, wait and see. I'll enjoy interrogating you. But for the time being, it's enough to know that you and your scummy friend are back, and safely under lock and key."

"Which was the main purpose of your visit, I take it? You can't have expected Crime and Security to just hand us over? Are you really sure that you don't want to talk about Lemnos…and *sqot*…and, er, the settlers…the Outsiders…oh yes, and whatever *Guardian Rebek'a* has to do with all that? As I said, we're definitely quite bored in here."

"That's all nonsense, Milliya, at least your version of events is. There'll be a time and a place for these matters to be clarified, and between now and then a lot can happen. You'll be transferred out of here soon enough, and then the interrogation can begin properly. Sleep on that, Milliya, if you can."

Having said her piece, Guardian Julieta left, undramatically, with Guardian Jeena (or was it Trainee Guardian

Jeena?) in her wake. Burk was almost sad to see her go. Milliya was pretty enough, yes, but *that* one!

Still, it was good that the two Guardians, when they left, weren't taking Burk and Milliya with them.

"May I wake you from your reverie, Mr. Burk? Would it help to wean you off Little Miss Pretty-as-a-Picture if I told you what trainees in Ideology like her are taught to do? With their bare hands? To men like you? I could even show you if you like!"

Burk declined the offer. She gave him another of the prearranged microsignals, meaning "Don't talk!"

Why not? A few seconds later he realized. As they both listened, without making a sound, they heard faint noises outside the room, the sound of several people shouting, and then a door being slammed. A disagreement among the Guardians!

The cell wasn't completely soundproof. That was good to know, Burk thought, because it meant that it wasn't intended to double as a torture chamber. Perhaps they should aim at staying there a bit longer…

He didn't share the thought with Milliya. There was probably no need—she was usually quicker on the up-take than he was.

Once again the door opened. Pigface and Mr. Sensitive came in. Pigface served them the drinks they had been promised (flat-tasting water with a strong hint of chemical additives) while Mr. Sensitive started clearing away the remains of their DELICIO banquet. He took his time over it, so that he was still stacking up the little containers on his tray when Pigface left the room.

"They wanted to take you with them," he whispered, "but the boss said 'no'."

Who was the boss? Doubtless someone who had the Government's interests at heart, rather than theirs. But anyone who could keep them out of the clutches of Guardian Rebek'a was a welcome friend.

"When will we...?"

Milliya gave him her sweetest look, the one she always used when she was wheedling and persuading (and a look with which Burk was all too familiar). It didn't fail this time either.

"I don't know. When she gets back, maybe."

She? Did he mean Guardian Sousanna?

"Might I ask you for a small favor, Colleague?"

This was pushing it too far.

"No."

But Milliya didn't give up.

"Could you switch off the machines for just half an hour, perhaps, so that we can have some privacy? You're a man of the world, you know what I mean!"

"Nope, I can't do that." He had fallen straight into the trap. Too late, he tried to repair the damage. "Machines? What machines?" He paused. "But I'll bring you a big blanket."

CHAPTER TWO

EATING, CUDDLING, BUT NOT
WATCHING A MOVIE

The "bed" was far from comfortable, but Burk and Milliya didn't mind once they were under the huge blanket that Mr. Sensitive had organized for them. They slept surprisingly well, and treated themselves to the luxury of a lie-in, which was disturbed only by the arrival of Pigface with a tray of the synthetic muck that passed for breakfast.

Where had Mr. Sensitive found the blanket? Why should anyone keep a large, warm blanket, a blanket with an attractive red, brown and black geometric design, moreover—as Milliya pointed out to him—in a gloomy place like this? They were still in the Crime and Security wing at the Space Disembarkation Terminal, in a short-term holding cell.

Correction, "short-term" must surely mean "very short-term," because the cell was barely furnished: apart from the bed, which had had no coverings on it, there was only a rickety table, and a single equally rickety chair. If Burk had been roughed up by the Guardians here in the cell, those items of furniture wouldn't have survived his being thrown against them for very long.

And there was no toilet. Every time one of them needed to "go", they had to thump on the door and shout for a

Guardian to escort them to the stinking latrine at the end of the corridor. This was a facility that in Milliya's opinion was principally used by the Guardians themselves. Dirty people, she said. No, this particular accommodation was intended only for very short-stay guests. As she explained, the personnel at any properly run prison, detention or interrogation center would go berserk if they were constantly required to attend to their customers' basic needs in this way. That wasn't what attracted you to a career in the Guardians.

Besides, she went on, an en suite bathroom such as you would expect a cell to have—in practice it would be a filthy little throne and a grimy wash basin—could also be a useful accessory for Phase 1 torture. He didn't know what that was? Better known as "softening up," it was a process that involved breaking down the prisoner's confidence and self-esteem. You used such tricks as sleep deprivation, enforced nakedness and verbal abuse, or petty humiliations like making the guy drink from the toilet or eat his own excrement. Entertaining enough, if you happened to enjoy that kind of work.

Burk was disconcerted.

"You're not cheering me up. And how do you know all this?"

"All part of the training."

Very well, he asked, if she was so clever what was going to happen to them next?

Now that was something she *didn't* know. The only answer was to wait and see. They didn't have any pressing social engagements, did they? They weren't obliged to be anywhere specific that morning, were they? Though most other places, almost any other dump you could think of, would have been preferable to the place they were presently in.

It was Crime and Security who had taken them, she said, but they didn't know what to do with them.

Their unsavory colleagues from Ideology would like to have them, but (fortunately!) they hadn't been able to countermand the original detention order.

There were two people who *did* have clear, and very different, ideas about what ought to be done with them, Guardian Sousanna and Guardian Rebek'a, and they were probably both still on their way back to Terra.

Burk was alarmed that she was talking so freely. They now knew that the cell was bugged.

"Is it wise...?"

"Oh, let them listen in if they want to. I think what happened during the visit that we had yesterday, from Guardian Julieta and her playmate, made the situation perfectly obvious. *Obvious to everyone.* Wouldn't you agree?"

That last question, he realized, wasn't necessarily aimed at Burk.

They would be stuck there, she opined, swallowing crappy Delicio products and shagging under the blanket, until one or other of the big guns turned up. She hoped that it would be Guardian Sousanna who got there first. If they arrived at the same time, there would be a galactic-scale ding-dong. It would be the girl-fight to end all girl-fights. And wouldn't that be fun? She knew which of them *she* would be cheering for.

If that was her attempt at humor, Burk didn't appreciate it.

"If Rebek'a gets here first, we're both dead. And we'll be lucky if we're only tasered."

Unusually, Milliya agreed with him.

"Yes, well done, quite right: I think that's our position put in a nutshell. What they might do to us *before* the tasering—well, I've seen rather more of that kind of thing than you have—"

"I beg your pardon, I haven't seen *any* of 'that kind of thing', and I don't want to start seeing it now. Especially at close range. And especially if I'm involved."

"Since there's not much we can do about it, darling, I suggest that we just lie back and enjoy the holiday camp. Because nothing's going to happen to us in here, is it? A pity that the food's so lousy, though. What about another cuddle?"

"I'm not in the mood."

"My poor dear has a headache, does he? Then boredom, I fear, is now on the agenda. I don't see an entertainment center anywhere in the room, do you? How unfortunate. We could have watched a movie. We could have watched your old friend Gloriya in one of her great roles: Nurse Meggan in *Kill for Love*, perhaps?"

Burk had to laugh at the thought of Gloriya in that awful movie, bursting pneumatically out of her costume, all bust and buttocks, and being lustfully abused (approximately every twenty minutes) by the loathsome Dr. Fell. Just before the end of the film, Nurse Meggan was surgically dismembered by the wicked doctor. The sensory effects had been particularly gross. Burk had always preferred his orgasms to be natural rather than electronically simulated.

"Not *that* film, please."

"Well, I think that's the only sort of movie that Gloriya ever made. But we haven't got that option anyway. And they haven't given us an information monitor either.

Withholding *that* from a smart young Media Studies graduate like yourself—whatever next?"

For once, Milliya was completely wrong, if she believed that their present captors wouldn't be doing anything. As indeed they were soon to find out. Or had she, by her chatter, deliberately been trying to provoke the Guardians into action? Wasn't it better to see what your enemy was doing, to have them doing it out there in the open in front of you, rather than wait and speculate about what they might be brewing up in the murk behind the scenes?

But were Pigface and her Guardian colleagues the "enemy" that they really needed to worry about?

What was presumably morning, midday and afternoon passed uneventfully, the intervals of time defined for them only by the regular appearance of meals, such as these were. It was surprising how many flavors the Delicio Corporation had managed to create that all tasted the same.

Burk and Milliya had effectively lost their sense of time. They had been in the pods for the final burst of interstellar high slide that took them into the solar system, and then on to their home planet; they had both been beaten up; and they had been stripped of all their personal electronic devices, with the various digital timekeeping possibilities that these offered. What they had briefly seen outside, through the windows of the Terminal, hadn't helped either—Terra, crushed for centuries by smog and pollution, was now dark and gloomy most of the time, day or night, even in what used to be called summer.

It must have been late afternoon or early evening when the Guardians came for them. Pigface was the only one that they recognized, and it was with some relief that

Burk saw from the insignia on their uniforms that the others were all from Crime and Security, and not from Ideology.

To the accompaniment of much exaggerated grunting, shoving, and waving of stun-clubs and tasers, they were frogmarched out of their cell and down the outside corridor, though (to their relief) in the other direction from the smelly latrine—that was a tiny piece of good news, for a start!

After rounding several corners they were brought to a halt outside a room, marked "X-12," which had an unusually impressive door. It was extremely solidly built, of expensive, carefully chosen material, quite unlike the cheap standardized doors that you otherwise saw in Government buildings and offices. The edges of the door neatly overlapped the lintel and the sides of the doorway. Burk, who had worked in various departments of Social and Recreational, knew what this could mean. Soundproofed doors normally led to a room designed for important purposes, like a ceremonial chamber or a conference hall.

There was another, less appealing, possibility: since they were in Crime and Security, this could also be the interrogation room.

Pigface keyed in a pass-code, and the door slid gently open, without the usual whirring and shuddering. Aha, Burk thought, an important room that they've spent some money on, a place for fancy events. Good!

But then his heart sank, because what they found when they were pushed inside the room tended to support his second theory.

There were tables and chairs, yes, and there was recording equipment, but also a tall, severe-looking Grade

III Guardian in a well-tailored uniform. He was standing stiffly against one of the tables, and spread out behind and to either side of him was a selection of sinister-looking gadgets and devices.

Could this be the "boss", who, according to Mr. Sensitive, had prevented Guardian Julieta from dragging them off to the dungeons of Ideology the night before? Burk couldn't imagine that the gadgets and devices were there for decoration. They weren't hobby items or toys, except in the sense that some Guardians might enjoy playing with them.

So they were in a torture chamber after all.

CHAPTER THREE

BURK AND MILLIYA ARE SHOWN
THE INSTRUMENTS

Pigface lined them up in front of the Grade III. He gestured to the Guardians to step back, as if to say that he didn't need anyone to protect him against the two detainees, even though they hadn't been handcuffed or bound. His whole manner oozed competence and self-confidence. True, it was harder for men to rise through the ranks of the Guardians, and those who did were often exceptionally able. But the message he was sending was that he was a man who could take them both out, without any help, if he wanted to.

"I'm not obliged to identify myself, but I will do. I am Guardian Grade III Selwin of the Crime and Security Section."

"Then you'll know—"

"Stop! You'll speak only when I tell you to, and when you do you'll address me as 'Guardian'. And you," he turned his icy gaze on Burk, "you will address me as 'sir'. Is that understood?"

They both nodded.

He explained to them that (among his other duties) he was in overall command of the Crime and Security detachment at the Space Disembarkation Terminal. He knew Guardian Sousanna very well, and had often worked with her. A highly efficient colleague! It was on her orders (she had recently been promoted to Grade IV, on a temporary basis, did they know that?)—

"No, Guardian." (Burk merely shook his head.)

—it was on her orders that they had been detained. *Detained*, not arrested, they should note, although there were warrants out against both of them, involving quite serious charges. Guardian Sousanna was now on her way back from Lemnos, on the people transporter *Starsearcher*, and she would probably be arriving at the Terminal the following day.

"However, Guardian Grade III Rebek'a from Ideology is also on the *Starsearcher*, and Guardian Sousanna has been unable to have her arrested, despite my colleague's recent temporary promotion." Guardian Sousanna's new status did seem to irk him slightly. "We may conclude from this that powerful people have taken Guardian Rebek'a under their protection. Do you know anything about that?"

"No, Guardian, I don't. I'm just a simple Grade I. And Burk, he's just an AdPop. We don't understand these higher matters."

"Don't play the innocent; you don't fool me for one moment! You were Guardian Rebek'a's lover, if that's the right word for it"—behind them, there was sniggering, and someone muttered "fuck toy"—"and lovers are known to whisper things to each other. Pillow-talk, I believe it's called?"

"She doesn't know anything, sir! Rebek'a never trusted anyone. She just used her—"

He broke off, in pain, as one of the Guardians (Pigface perhaps?) kicked him viciously from behind in response to a gesture from the "boss".

"Yes, I'm sure that Guardian Rebek'a *used* her, and in ways that you or I can barely imagine!" There was more sniggering. He turned to Milliya. "I have to say, my dear, that you have a peculiar taste in sexual partners: first a vicious lesbian, and then a pathetic AdPop. But if you still value him, and would like him to stay in one piece, make it clear to him that he is not to speak unless he's asked to."

"Yes, Guardian. I think he understands that now."

Burk was still hurting, but he couldn't help noticing the hint of a smirk on her face. He could guess what she was thinking: here's a male Guardian who's made it up the ranks, but he's still unsure of himself, he still has to go on proving that he's just as hard as the girls.

That made him insecure, fair enough; it didn't necessarily make him sadistic, or unreasonable.

"As I said, Guardian Sousanna sent instructions, and that is why we are here now." He turned to Burk. "Do you know what these things are? *She* knows. And she knows what we're doing now." There was no answer. "Go ahead. You can speak now."

Burk looked at Milliya, who nodded to him in encouragement.

"They're tasers. I think. Some of them, anyway."

"Not bad, for an AdPop. Some of them *are* tasers. But look carefully. What do you see that's different about them?"

Burk looked at the tasers. They did seem rather elaborate, with gaudily-colored attachments and fiddly controls. And they were larger, and no doubt heavier, than standard tasers were. They wouldn't be very effective in a street fight or a riot. Could they be the old kind, which he'd once seen in a museum, the sort that had conductor wires to carry the charge? That was unlikely, because some of them had digital display panels.

He thought it best not to say anything.

"*You* tell him, then. You've seen them before; he hasn't."

Milliya leaned towards Burk, and spoke in a quiet voice.

"These are not ordinary tasers. Ordinary tasers have three normal settings: 'WARNING', 'SEDATION', and 'HIGH'. And there is a fourth setting, 'CIRCUIT BREAKER', which is used with androids. The 'HIGH' setting is selected only to kill someone. For 'SEDATION', there's an additional dial that you can turn from 'LOW' through 'MEDIUM' and 'HIGH' all the way up to 'MAXIMUM'. 'HIGH SEDATION' and 'MAXIMUM SEDATION' can both be deadly, depending on the victim's age, body weight, and state of health. But if you want to be sure, you set the switch to 'HIGH'. That's *always* fatal. It takes a while to get used to this, and nobody wants to make a mistake, so most Guardians keep 'LOW SEDATION' as the default setting. That wouldn't kill anyone, except a small child or a bad cardiac case."

Guardian Selwin applauded ironically.

"Well done, my dear. You would have made a fine Guardian trainer. But if these aren't normal tasers, what are they?"

Milliya sucked in her breath.

"These are torture tasers."

Guardian Selwin tut-tutted in irritation.

"Now now, that won't do at all. Not torture—you mean *interrogation* tasers. I hope that you always used the correct term when dealing with suspects?"

Milliya didn't answer that at first, but Burk thought to himself that the subtleties of terminology wouldn't matter much to any poor swine who was having the device used on him.

"Yes, Guardian, of course: interrogation tasers, that's what I meant to say."

"And how are they different from normal tasers?"

"Normal tasers are used to disable or sedate, or to kill. Interrogation tasers are used only to cause pain."

"You mean: disorientation, followed by gradations of physical discomfort. Let's get the terminology right, if we can."

"Yes, Guardian."

"Do continue."

"They are designed to be applied to specific parts of the body such as the forehead, nipples, hands or genitals. You need to choose the right device to achieve optimal interrogation results."

"That is true. And?"

"The controls are more complicated. But that doesn't matter, because there is no hurry—the settings can be adjusted at leisure."

"And what settings are we talking about?"

"There are settings to direct different kinds of shock or pulse to different areas of the nervous system, sometimes several at the same time, irrespective of how the device is positioned. There are also settings that can modulate the length, repetition, and intensity of the...*discomfort*. The newest models can even lower the suspect's discomfort threshold in general, although I suspect that in practice many interrogators still prefer to do that in the old-fashioned way, using tried and tested methods."

"Which are?"

"Pharmaceuticals."

Milliya was warming to her subject.

"Not bad—but you've forgotten something."

"Of course: the interrogation taser also monitors and records the suspect's metabolic reactions."

"Why is that important?"

"Because you don't want to give the suspect a heart attack or a stroke, or knock him or her unconscious, do you?"

"Bravo! That pretty well covers everything. And your overall opinion of this equipment?"

Milliya's eyes gleamed. Burk dearly hoped that she was only play-acting, but he couldn't be certain.

"Wonderful! It's a remarkable piece of engineering. These devices provide the Guardian interrogator with an unparalleled range of options with regard to discomfort delivery…"

Was it now her turn to be ironic, or was she just quoting the boastful statement at the beginning of the manufacturers' instruction handbook?

"Good. I see that we are in agreement. Shall we now *try out* the tasers on one of you?"

To her credit, Milliya said nothing.

Burk swallowed hard, but he had been expecting from the first moment that they saw the tasers laid out on the table that eventually the situation was going to move in that direction. Towards *pain*.

There was only one way out of this. Burk did the bravest thing he had ever done in his life: he laughed.

"I don't think you will, sir, if you'll excuse my saying so!"

CHAPTER FOUR

BURK'S DEGREE IN LIBERAL ARTS (MEDIA STUDIES) PROVES TO BE USEFUL

Everyone around him stiffened. He could sense Milliya screaming silently: "No, no, no, are you completely crazy?" He knew that he was trembling, and tried to control it. They were no longer pinioned, but he half-expected the pack of Guardians ranged behind them to now leap onto them, kicking, punching, and gouging.

Guardian Selwin turned on Burk the whole cold venom of his Guardian Death Look. It would have shriveled him up completely...if he hadn't already experienced (and survived) Guardian Rebek'a's terrifying version of the same.

Were the Guardians actually trained to do this, using old Japanese samurai movies and Eisenstein films? Burk had done a seminar on twentieth-century cinema on his Media Studies degree course, and later he'd been put in charge of a movie library, with lots of classic films that no-one (except himself) ever wanted to watch.

"I will do whatever I like to your miserable AdPop carcass, Mr. Burk, and you'll be surprised what that may include."

The "mister" was not an expression of politeness. But Burk knew what he was doing (he hoped!), and what did they have to lose?

"I'm sure you're right, sir. But with all due respect: *it won't be today.*"

"And why not?"

"Because you won't authorize it before Guardian Sousanna has returned."

Guardian Selwin goggled at him in amazement, momentarily lost for words. Milliya reached out and tapped his arm.

"Burk!" she whispered urgently.

Yet for once he was a step ahead of her. Yes, of course he knew that Guardian Selwin resented the promotion enjoyed by his colleague, who was now his boss. And of course he was aware that, by reminding him of her new seniority, he was rubbing the man's nose in it (those wonderful old metaphors that you only got from books!). But he also knew what to say next.

It *had* to work. He was staking everything on one throw of the dice (another metaphor!).

"You won't authorize it, sir, because"—and he paused, since timing was everything—"you are doing something different, something very well thought out, that could get you the same results with less work and fewer risks."

"Am I?"

"You are, sir. And I only realized it by chance, because of what I studied at college. Otherwise I would never have guessed."

Guardian Selwin snorted contemptuously.

"Pah! What you studied at college? Media Studies, with a Minor in Literature? I don't see the relevance."

"But it was in Liberal Arts, sir, and we did lots of history! And back then, in olden times, in the Middle Ages, you know, the Spanish Inquisition—"

"I *don't* know, Burk, and why don't I? Because I studied Advanced Cybernetics, a useful subject, and not that kind of nonsense. So get to the point, and stop wasting my time!"

"Well, back then, before they tortured anyone—sorry, *interrogated* them—they used to show them the instruments, and explain what they were capable of doing. Or, even better than that, they asked them to guess how they thought the instruments worked. It was called The Question. It was very effective. A lot of people shat themselves and confessed straight away. Or maybe the following day, after a dreadful, sleepless night, of course. And that's what you've been doing with us. A very efficient approach. Guardian Sousanna would never have thought of it."

He had almost said "clever," but that would have been a mistake. No, for a cyberneticist "efficient" was the right word.

But he was wrong about Guardian Sousanna.

Guardian Selwin seemed to take the bait.

"Well, well, well, Mr. Burk, my oh my, how we've underestimated you! You have seen right through me." He paused, pursing his lips thoughtfully. "Of course I had no intention of beginning the interrogation without Guardian Sousanna. That would have been most unprofessional. She is on her way here with information about you that we don't happen to have. But you are quite right—it can be helpful to prepare the subjects beforehand, to make them aware of what is coming. So: now that we all know what we are doing, why don't we continue with The Question? You didn't do very well with the tasers. Perhaps you might explain the other items to us? You may even handle them if you like."

Burk hadn't seen that coming. He approached the table and picked up the first device that clearly wasn't a taser.

"The settings on this are…for temperature, so it must be for causing burns. Am I right, sir?"

"It's somewhat more sophisticated than that, but, yes, essentially that is what it does."

That was an easy one. Next he picked up what might have been a large glove, with openings for the fingers and the thumb. Each of the openings was lined with a soft pad, from which, however, sharp wedges protruded.

"This is for crushing the flesh of the fingers, but also for breaking individual bones, by means of these wedges."

"Correct. And the syringes in that box?"

"Are for administering drugs to induce discomfort or nausea, or make the prisoner feel disoriented. Maybe truth drugs, too?"

"No, we don't use those very much. It's difficult to get the dosage right. If you inject too little, Guardians like your friend here would know how to block it by applying simple autogenic techniques. Your miserable namesake Ciaran Burke taught his followers how to do that using yoga. Evil is so inventive! If you inject too much, on the other hand, the subject becomes a raging pyschotic. Still, I think it might work with *you*. Why are you smiling?"

"Oh, nothing in particular, sir. Just tiredness. We were in the pods. Stress…"

"No, go ahead. Something made you smile."

Burk couldn't resist.

"It's just the historian in me, sir. We think we're *so* advanced. We think we're *so* developed. But we're still interrogating people the way they did centuries ago:

burning them, breaking their bones, giving them electric shocks."

Guardian Selwin glowered at him.

"Rubbish! You talk like a stupid Ciaranite. And don't underestimate what we can do. But though you prattle a lot, I don't think you know very much. You're just an Ad-Pop with ideas above his station, and you've been playing for time with all this crap about the Middle Ages. *She's* the one that we want to talk to. Perhaps we shouldn't wait, either. After all, it might be Guardian *Rebek'a* who comes and collects her tomorrow, in person. Her people have already tried once." He rubbed his hands together suggestively. "You know, I think that we might undertake some softening up after all. It doesn't have to be psychological. She might tell us something; and with *you* it would just be for fun."

Burk sensed the Guardians moving towards them, but then Milliya, as if on cue, tottered, whispered "Oh dear", and slumped dramatically to the ground.

Pigface attended to her with surprising gentleness. She carried Milliya to a chair, wiped her forehead with an impregnated cloth, and squirted some medicinal elixir into her with a nasal spray.

Milliya groaned and muttered, but her words were incomprehensible.

"Let me take her to the medical room, Guardian. I can have her ready for you in twenty minutes."

But Guardian Selwin had already lost interest. It was late, he was tired, and the prisoners wouldn't be going anywhere. They could wait until the morning, but they must be woken very early, so that he could have a crack at them before Guardian Sousanna (or the other one) showed up.

The equipment should be taken back to his office. Guardian Sirina (that was Pigface) could bring the prisoners to him, along with his breakfast, before she went off shift. He liked to begin the day with light refreshment and something mildly diverting.

Then he left, without wishing anyone "good night".

Burk and Milliya were trundled back to their cell and locked in. They had a lot to think about—and worry about—but Milliya was still groggy, and battling to stay awake. She hugged Burk and told him that she had to sleep.

"You do know that I love you, don't you? Whatever happens. And whatever you know, or *think* that you know, don't tell them anything."

She repeated that she loved him; and then she closed her eyes and slept.

It took Burk longer to fall asleep, tormented as he was by fear of what might be done to them the next day.

They woke simultaneously, and with a start. There were muffled sounds from outside. Something was going on out in the corridor.

They had no way of telling the time, but Burk felt only half-refreshed, as you do when you are shaken out of sleep prematurely, so he guessed that it must still be night.

Why the commotion outside?

Milliya hugged him tightly.

"I *do* love you, Burk."

Then the door opened, and they were dazzled by the light from outside, against which several dark figures were silhouetted. There was shouting, and someone was screaming. Was there a fight going on? Were they being rescued? They huddled back under the blanket. The figures weren't dark, they were *black*. They were dressed in black fatigues, and wearing masks. They carried machetes in their hands. Burk had seen them before—on Lemnos. The Outsiders!

So Guardian Rebek'a had got to them first after all, though not in the way that they'd expected.

One of the figures approached them.

"Get up, you're coming with us."

Burk had absolutely no wish to do that, and he was therefore surprised when Milliya almost sprang to her feet.

"Come on, Burk!"

Why was she so keen? Guardian Rebek'a might spare Milliya, for old time's sake, but for him this would mean death, and not a pleasant one.

Rather incongruously, he found himself shouting "Who is authorizing this? Where is Guardian Selwin?" (Why did he say that? The guy had been planning to torture him. But Guardian Selwin still represented law and order, and doing things by the book.)

The man in black laughed, and half-turned, calling out to the figures behind him, "He means the Boss Man, I reckon! Which of you guys has got Guardian Selwin? Bring him here!"

Someone threw a bulky object towards Burk, so that it landed at his feet. It was Guardian Selwin. But not the whole of him—just his severed head.

"There he is! I don't think he wants to talk to *you*, though. Now: move!"

They were hauled out of the cell. Outside there was complete mayhem. Several dead Guardians lay in the corridor, where they had been chopped down. There was blood on the floor, and smears of blood on the walls. Burk stared in horror at the bodies. Pigface was lying on her back, but he only recognized her by the two red shoulder slashes on her uniform—her face had been hacked off with a machete.

"Hurry, hurry, the new shift is coming and the pass-codes willl be changed!" A small, energetic black figure bustled about, and seemed to be in charge. He waved towards Burk. "No, stop, put him back in the cell. That one stays here! There isn't room in the transporter for him."

Burk thought his voice was familiar, but who could it be? He wasn't one of the Outsiders from Lemnos. But then, as the man turned away and Burk saw him side-on, saw his hunched shoulders under the black jacket, he realized: it was the Scribe Jacoob! How could he be an Outsider?

"Jacoob? Why aren't you taking me as well?"

Now the little man looked at him, but the eyes that gleamed through the holes in the mask were cold.

"Oh, Mr. Burk, what a pity. You've spoilt everything. You should have stayed in bed. Give me a taser, someone. Quickly."

Milliya threw herself between them.

"No, stop, you can't do that!"

"Can't I? Shut her up!"

A dark figure slipped a cloth over her face from behind and pulled it taut, choking and gagging her. Then she was dragged away.

"We were planning to leave you here, Mr. Burk. You are surplus to our requirements, to *anyone's* requirements, and our little transporter will be full. But now that you've seen through our masquerade, we can't leave you here *alive*, can we?" He fiddled with the taser, then spoke to one of his men. "Is this a new model? Ah, that's what I was looking for: 'HIGH'. Goodbye, Mr. Burk. When you meet Death, pass on my regards."

And then he fired straight into Burk, point-blank.

CHAPTER FIVE

BURK IN THE AFTERLIFE

People who've had near-death experiences say that, when you die, you find yourself traveling down a long, curving tunnel towards a bright light. You feel euphoric. They can't tell you much about what comes next, though according to some who claim to know more it involves meeting God, St. Peter, or an angel. Or someone unpleasant from the Other Place.

When you're tasered to death it's not like that. Your body disintegrates. Every nerve is incinerated, and sends a shock wave hammering against the next nerve. The shock has nowhere to go, like an explosion in a narrow tunnel, and it turns into pain such as you could never have imagined until it actually happens to you.

The pain doesn't go away—it shrieks and howls and tears you apart. If you were outside it, you would know that it only takes a few seconds before you die; when you are inside it, when the pain is inside *you*, consuming you whole, it feels like an eternity. Is that maybe where the idea of hell comes from?

Burk was dead. The pain had ceased, so now he must be in the afterlife. The light was bright, yet restful, and not like the flashing and burning that had accompanied the pain. He felt pleasantly comfortable. Where was the euphoria, though? That was a disappointment.

An angel was bending over him, looking into his face. She was of great beauty, but very stern. Was this an angel of judgment? He didn't know what to say. Could he justify his life? Probably he had wasted it, but he hadn't been a truly bad person. He couldn't remember ever doing anything wicked *deliberately*, though there were one or two girls he hadn't treated too well (though far more girls who'd treated *him* badly). "More sinned against than sinning." Where was that from? Being dead obviously wasn't good for your memory.

Maybe the angel was waiting for him to say something in his defence. Was there any need? The recording angels would have told her everything, wouldn't they?

"I haven't been a very moral person," he croaked penitently. "I've done some bad things in my life, I know that."

The angel slapped his face.

"Wake up, Burk, and talk sense!"

It wasn't an angel. It was Guardian Sousanna.

"Oh. So I'm not dead?"

No, he wasn't. It was definitely Guardian Sousanna looming over him so imperiously, and in the background practical, everyday things were going on—cleaning, wiping, swabbing, carrying and rearranging of furniture—stuff that you wouldn't expect the angels in heaven to be doing.

"I'm sure you've done some bad things, Burk, but you didn't do *this*."

She made a sweeping gesture with her hand, taking in the scene of carnage behind her.

"No."

"I count six dead Guardians, four of them grossly mutilated. They were colleagues of mine. Someone is going to pay for this! And one missing prisoner. You can't have done this, Burk, unless you tasered yourself afterwards?" He didn't reply. "That was a rhetorical question."

"Milliya's gone. *They* took her. Then they tried to kill me."

She held up a taser, which looked not unlike the one that Scribe Jacoob had used on him.

"With this, by any chance?" He nodded. "Well, *there's* a little mystery. It's set to 'HIGH', and that would have been enough to kill an elephant (if you remember elephants?). Except that this is not a standard taser, it's an interrogation taser, and on this kind of device 'HIGH' doesn't mean 'kill'. It means: 'cause maximum pain'. *Was* it painful, Burk?"

He licked his lips, and remembered.

"Oh yes."

"That's a strange mistake for someone to make, don't you think? Assuming that they *wanted* to kill you. And it wouldn't have been made by someone familiar with tasers, someone who knew how to use them. Someone like Guardian Rebek'a."

Burk's mouth was horribly dry. His brain was now working in turbo mode—he had to be very, very careful what he said.

"It wasn't Guardian Rebek'a," he croaked. "It was an ugly great man in a black uniform, wearing a black mask."

"Yes, one of Rebek'a's Outsider friends. We found an abandoned mask in the outer corridor. Our forensic team is now taking a look at it. The costumes, the machetes and mutilations—it all fits a clear pattern. It couldn't have been Rebek'a personally, though, because she has an alibi. She was disembarking from the *Starsearcher* at the time, and I never let her out of my sight."

"They took Milliya. By force. She didn't go willingly. Why didn't they take me as well?"

She laughed, though not unpleasantly. Everything that Guardian Sousanna did was done with style, and with efficiency. She was highly professional. With her there would never be any unnecessary nastiness, he was sure, never any unnecessary violence.

"My dear Burk, the really interesting question is: why did they *take* Milliya, instead of just killing her? At the moment, I see two feasible explanations. One possibility is this: next month there is going to be a public enquiry into this whole murky business of Lemnos, and *sqot*. Milliya may have incriminating material—data, recordings, some soil samples—which she's hidden somewhere. If that's the case, they will be tickling its wherabouts out of her right now, so that they can find and destroy it, but they'll keep her alive until they've achieved that. Do you happen to know of any such material?"

He shook his head.

"Guardian Rebek'a made her hand over her communicator—"

"—which I was unable to confiscate, unfortunately."

Burk almost ruined it by laughing. The communicator that Milliya had thrown to her was not her own, it was Aylwin's, and contained only the settler's home-made bondage movies, in each of which Aylwin himself played the leading role. Rebek'a would have found them most diverting!

"Guardian Rebek'a may have had personal reasons for sparing her life. She and Milliya…"

He stopped, unwilling to continue. Guardian Sousanna spared him that embarrassment.

"Yes, *very* personal reasons, Burk—I know all about those goings on. Rebek'a is many things, but she's not sentimental, and there are other pretty girls out there, so I suspect a different purpose. My second theory is that she was hoping to turn Milliya again, and then use her as a witness against us at the enquiry, with or without any evidence that she might have."

"Then why didn't they take me too, for the same reason?"

Again, that gentle laughter, the kindly laughter of a teacher who is amused that her pupil is so slow on the uptake.

"What use would you be to them? If they have Milliya as a witness, they don't need an *AdPop's* testimony to corroborate hers. Neither would your testimony bear much weight if it contradicted her evidence. So they didn't need you."

He remembered what Jacoob had said.

"Surplus to requirements."

"I beg your pardon?" Guardian Sousanna looked surprised. "Where did you pick up *that* phrase? But, yes, I suppose you're right."

"They didn't need to kill me, though, did they? Not if no-one is going to listen to my evidence anyway."

"Don't get me wrong, Burk: people will certainly listen to you—as I'm listening to you now—but your testimony on its own won't carry much weight against the testimony of a Guardian. Trying to kill you was personal, though. From on-board the *Starsearcher*, Rebek'a must have found some way to contact her friends and tell them to eliminate you, and to do it as painfully as possible.

She might have preferred to have you to herself for a few hours, to play with you, but if you're in a hurry, tasering offers the ideal combination of speed and cruelty. You're just very lucky that, whoever it was she gave those instructions to, that person picked the wrong sort of taser."

One of her team of Guardians came and crouched beside her. She whispered into Guardian Sousanna's ear, and they had a brief conversation, of which Burk picked up only isolated words. "Office" and "taser" were two of them.

He needed to be very careful. Why should he tell them everything that he knew? Guardian Rebek'a and the Outsiders were thoroughly evil, and they had to be stopped. If letting the Government think that they were responsible for the massacre would help achieve that, then so be it!

For the immediate future, Milliya was in comparatively safe hands. The Ciaranites would protect her. But that didn't mean that she was out of danger. The Ciaranites had shown how ruthless they could be, and as for the Government: if they thought that Milliya had become a Ciaranite, her life was as good as over. Her name would go on a death-list, and it wouldn't be long before special agents found and terminated her.

And she wouldn't be terribly popular with Guardian Rebek'a's friends either.

The Ciaranites would want to use her information, primarily against Guardian Rebek'a and the Outsiders, rather than against the Government. Though how would they do it? They certainly wouldn't be showing up at the public enquiry! "Hello, we're terrorists, and we'd like to take part." But there were other ways to spread information—the media set-up on Terra was a soup of overlapping and conflicting providers that no-one could properly supervise. It would be easy to put out information and then switch to another media site, before the Government had even been able to close down the first source.

The brutality of the Ciaranites had shocked him. It worried him deeply that Jacoob had been so unconcerned about killing him. Wasn't the little Scribe supposed to be one of the good guys?

"Time to get up, Burk, if you feel strong enough? Ouch! I've been kneeling here for so long my legs have gone to sleep."

Burk started. That was almost the first personal comment that he had ever heard her make. Otherwise, she was always Pallas Athene: aloof, and dignified, like a Greek goddess in cold marble. So she was a human being after all!

"Yes, I can walk. I think…"

His legs were weak, though, and without much feeling in them. She steered him towards a chair, just before his legs gave way under him, and then parked herself on another chair beside him. A Guardian brought him the rest of his clothes, and his shoes—he had been wearing very little when the attackers dragged him from the cell—and even helped him to put them on.

"The taser must have come from Guardian Selwin's office. There were two other interrogation tasers lying there on his desk. They should of course have been locked away in a cupboard. Had he already interrogated you, or Milliya? We couldn't find any recorded interrogation protocol."

"No, we weren't interrogated." (Which, strictly speaking, was true.)

"That's most irregular behavior on his part. They looted some of the equipment in his office, decoders, communicators and the like, and the Outsiders must have mistaken this taser for a standard one that they could use on you." Suddenly she looked thoughtful. "Does that mean that they broke in without combat tasers? I would have expected the Outsiders to be much better equipped. How strange! But once they were inside the Crime and Security building, if they moved quickly and caught the Guardians by surprise those machetes of theirs would have been more than sufficient."

Burk wasn't feeling too great. He was wondering where they'd be housing him next. In an underground dungeon? Or a torture chamber? Would they lock him, unconscious, in a Terran holding pod? Or freeze him in a cryogenic facility until they'd decided what to do with him? He was feeling distinctly sorry for himself.

"I suppose you're going to arrest me properly now. We did promise you, on Lemnos, that we'd present ourselves to your department to answer the charges against us. So, fair enough, that's what I'm doing now: I'm presenting myself. Besides, I don't think I could run away if I wanted to."

"No, Burk, I don't think you could! But we're not going to arrest you. The pedophile charges were a frame-up, as you well know. It was just so that we could stop you from disembarking at the Gate of Lemnos, and have you sent back to Terra. I'm sorry, but it was a necessary tactic, a temporary measure, and under urgent circumstances. Those charges will all be dropped. But the other charge—"

"What other charge?"

"The charge of twice falsifying your identity—once as the Adpop 'Markko Mann', and once as the Use-Pop 'Mytt'. That charge was not so easily disposed of, especially as you passed yourself off as a member of a higher social stratum. The punishment for that is ten years in an outer galactic mining colony. Would you survive that, Burk? I somehow doubt it. Those are not pleasant places."

"But you are going to drop that charge, too? You did use the past tense."

"Yes," she said, "if you co-operate with us the charge will be dropped. But an entry will remain in your record, so that you are effectively on probation."

"And what do I have to do?"

"Nothing. Enjoy your life, Burk. You're a free man. Outside that door is the Western American Megalopolis—your home. We request only that you stay at your known address, and that you report to us if you hear anything interesting. Or if anyone contacts you. If you are called to testify next month, you will testify, but it's unlikely that you'll be needed. How would it help us? Who would believe your word against hers?"

"Well, she's prettier than I am, no question of it."

Guardian Sousanna was not amused.

"Was that intended to be funny? I can see how you found your niche in Social and Recreational. You claim to have loved her. Then show some respect! They may be interrogating her—no, let's call things by their proper names—they may be *torturing* her as we speak. She may be a traitor. She may even be a murderer. But don't be flippant about her, Burk. That does you no credit."

"I'm sorry," he said, and he might have said more, feeling rather ashamed of himself as he now did, but he was distracted by a sudden bustle of talk and activity further down the corridor. A noticeably pretty Grade I hurried over to them She apologized for interrupting.

Squatting beside her boss, her uniform nicely tightened over her thighs, she whispered a fairly lengthy message to her.

If the news was surprising, or unexpected, Guardian Sousanna gave no indicaton of it. She listened, nodding several times, and when the girl had finished she gave her reply.

"Keep them waiting for half an hour. Tell them that the forensic people aren't quite finished. Then go and make sure that the forensic people *are* finished. Nothing of interest must be lying around for our visitors to touch or to see. Inform headquarters, and make it clear to them that the Minister herself should be told. Speak to her yourself if they let you."

"Yes, Guardian."

"Tell your colleagues to have their tasers set to 'LOW SEDATION', not switched off. They should form a reception party at the door. That'll be more for show—I don't expect there to be any violence, but you can never be sure. Give me a signal when everything is ready. Then, and only then, you may let them in." She turned to Burk, with a peculiar smile on her face that Burk would have described as "conspiratorial"—he didn't know what else it could be. "You were saying?"

"Look, do you want me to go back to my cell or something? I don't want to be in anybody's way."

Guardian Sousanna at first ignored his question.

"She's a bright one, that girl. Guardian Anfea. She's excellent leadership material: intelligent, reliable, level-headed. In fact, she's a bit like Milliya, before she went wrong. Of course I don't have favorites, the way that Guardian Rebek'a does, but *she's* definitely one to watch." She paused, then added nonchalantly: "Oh, and you can stay here, Burk, why not? It'll add to the fun. I ought to tell you: we have important visitors. Guardian Rebek'a herself is waiting outside, with her team from Ideology. She's come to collect the two prisoners, she says. *Her* prisoners. Well, well, what a surprise!"

CHAPTER SIX

WHEN GIRLS COLLIDE: RUN AND HIDE

The two Guardians, Sousanna and Rebek'a, had already crossed swords (metaphorically) on board the *Starstretcher*, at the hearing at which Burk had been wrongly accused of pedophilia.

They had crossed tasers (or at least they had pointed tasers at each other) on Lemnos, at the mysterious site on the Other Side where Guardian Rebek'a's sinister friends had been up to no good, stripping the soil with excavating machinery.

Burk was apprehensive about what might happen at their third encounter involving him! Would there be collateral damage? Burk, for example, if he got in the firing line?

Back in the early twenty-first century there had been a catchy popsong, *When Girls Collide: Run and Hide*, by a dreadful group called Ukelele. They were named after the unlikely favorite instrument of their charismatic frontman. Burk's then girlfriend, the one who had forced him to watch Gloriya movies on the entertainment center, loved that sort of music and was a mine of information (a rubbish tip of information?) about bands and musicians. Running and hiding was what Burk was now considering doing.

But he did neither. Quaking in his shoes and unsteady on his feet as he was, he would stand his ground—and he hoped that Guardian Sousanna would be able to protect him.

The Ciaranites had taken Milliya. But Guardian Rebek'a didn't know that. She wanted Milliya, and maybe she had an authorization to take her—she'd take Burk, too, as a bonus, a tasty morsel to play with, the way Burk had once seen a cat toying with a mouse, out of boredom or malice, but not hunger.

How would she react when she was told that Milliya was gone, and that her friends the Outsiders were suspected of snatching her? Would she believe it, or would she assume it was a trick and that Milliya was being withheld from her?

Guardian Sousanna too would be puzzled, and angered. Why had her colleague come? Was she misinformed? Had she come to gloat? Or was she playing some game of her own?

Burk was almost pleased that he knew more than either of the Guardians did. Or: he *would* have been pleased, if he hadn't been quite so frightened. For the moment, it would be safer for him not to reveal anything. Milliya wouldn't be popular with either side if there was any suspicion that she was helping or collaborating with the Ciaranites.

Ciaranites were known to have a very low life-expectancy.

The door opened, and Guardian Rebek'a marched in, as confidently as if she were walking into her own headquarters. Behind her, and struggling to keep up, was a line of Guardians from Ideology led by Guardian Julieta. They couldn't spread out threateningly as they might have liked to because, following the instructions she'd been given, Guardian Anfea had positioned the Crime and Security Guardians to either side of the visitors, forcing them to enter almost in single file and under the tasers of their hosts.

They were mostly big-boned, powerful-looking women, the normal Guardian physical type, but Guardian Rebek'a towered over all of them. The one exception, right at the back, was the slim figure of Miss Bee-sting. How did she get mixed up with *that* horrible lot? What a waste!

Burk couldn't help himself. Since he was no longer under the watchful eye of Milliya, he treated himself to an amiable leer at the delightful trainee. My, was she pretty!

Guardian Rebek'a came straight to the point.

"You have two detainees in your custody. I have here an order authorizing me to relieve you of responsibility for them. The prisoners are now a matter for Ideology, and no longer concern you."

As if to underscore what she was saying, she held out a communicator, waving it rudely under Guardian Sousanna's nose.

"May I see that, Colleague?"

"Of course you may. But please don't waste our time." She handed her the communicator. Spotting Burk, she said, "I see that the dog is here, so the bitch won't be far away?"

Burk pretended to be invisible.

Ignoring her colleague's last comment, Guardian Sousanna studied the display of the communicator, made a few adjustments to call up additional information, and then handed the device back.

"It's an Imperial Rescript. *Another* one." And she smiled. "But it's not from the Emperor Himself, is it? There is no voiceprint authentication, no electronic seal to indicate that. Or am I overlooking something?"

"It is signed by the Secretary to His Imperial Majesty's Advisory Council—"

"Yes, I know who that is. His Excellency Count Stelios Dagon. The same gentleman who signed the last one, too."

"His Excellency takes a keen interest in these matters."

"I'm sure he does. I have considerable respect for His Excellency—"

Guardian Rebek'a grunted. "And so you should." She seemed to be growing in size, as if to assert her increasing command of the situation by making herself bigger.

"No, don't get me wrong. I have a lot of respect for him, as a wise adviser to His Imperial Majesty, and as the hardworking Secretary to His Majesty's advisory council—all of whom, himself included, I should point out, are *unelected*." She enunciated the last word with obvious relish. "As we all know, however, an Imperial Rescript can't take the place of laws and ordinances that issue from the elected Government of Terra."

Guardian Rebek'a glared at her colleague, and waved the communicator as close as she could to her face without actually hitting her.

"Don't try to teach me constitutional law! Are you refusing to obey a Rescript? With or without the Imperial signature, this is binding."

"That is correct. But the function of Imperial Rescripts is not to *replace* the law, but merely to provide necessary decisions in ongoing situations, situations of confusion, perhaps, or panic. They remain valid only until a proper Government order has been issued."

"Exactly! I couldn't have explained it better myself. And this Rescript trumps any low-level detention warrant that you may have, I'll wager? Argue yourself out of *that* one, Miss Would-Be Lawyer! You know, Sousanna, you're so conceited, so convinced of your own intellectual superiority… I've always had an inclination to slap your smug face, but now you've saved me the trouble! Guardian Grade IV, *Provisional*. Don't make me laugh! But I think your career is about to suffer an embarrassing little downturn. It's time for you to do what you're told." She fixed her gaze on Burk. "We've established that one of the detainees is already here—someone fetch me the other one!"

Up to this point Guardian Sousanna had remained remarkably cool in the face of all this shouting and bullying. It may have helped that several of her Guardians' tasers were pointing straight at her aggressive colleague. Yet now for the first time she looked agitated, and her voice shook noticeably as she spoke.

"I don't know what game you're playing here, Rebek'a, but it's more than sick. Last night your friends, the same thugs that I met on Lemnos, abducted Guardian Milliya, and left the AdPop here for dead. They killed and mutilated my respected Grade III colleague Guardian Selwin, and they cut off the face of my Grade II unit commander. They have murdered every member of the Crime and Security team here at the Terminal. And now you come marching in here, huffing and puffing about taking charge of our prisoners—one of whom you already have, while the other your men nearly killed only a few hours ago!"

Guardian Rebek'a stared at her in amazement.

"I don't know what you're talking about."

Even if Burk *hadn't* known that her reaction was genuine, the expression on her face would still have convinced him.

"Oh yes you do! You're setting up a smokescreen, aren't you? Playing the innocent. This whole charade: what better way to make people think that you have nothing to do with what went on here last night?"

But Guardian Rebek'a was now also putting two and two together.

"You cunning bitch! I see what you're up to: you sacrifice a whole squadron of your own Guardians, so that you can hide Milliya away from me, *and* put the blame on me at the same time. Nicely done! And no doubt Milliya will miraculously reappear just in time for the enquiry. You didn't bother to hide the AdPop, because so long as you have *her* his evidence is irrelevant. But why not use him as a 'witness'" (she gave the word an ironic twist) "to the events that you staged here? After which he becomes disposable."

Burk didn't like the sound of that. For the third time in a few hours someone was saying that he was "surplus to requirements".

"You're right: Burk will have to give his account of what happened here last night."

"Well, don't worry about that, Colleague. He's coming with us now, and we'll take care of the interrogation. We have plenty of expertise in that particular area…"

Guardian Sousanna didn't reply.

Burk didn't know what to do. There was nowhere to hide. Two of the Ideology thugs were already moving towards him.

Suddenly Guardian Anfea stepped forward, holding out a communicator on which a little red light was flashing. A data transfer? An incoming call or message? She handed it to her boss.

"It's for you, Guardian. It's the call you were expecting."

"Not *more* time-wasting, Colleague? Haven't you organized enough cheap theatricals? It's time to go. Burk, you're coming with us!"

"No, stop. It's not for me—it's for you. It's the Minister. She wants to talk to you. In the matter of the Rescript."

Burk realized that she had played for time, and won— at least for now.

Guardian Rebek'a took the communicator from her and listened to what the Minister of Internal Security told her. A couple of times she said "Yes, ma'am" or "No, ma'am", her face blackenening with suppressed rage, but she had no choice but to obey.

There were ministers, and then again there were *ministers*. A department like African Affairs, for example, had no real clout, everyone knew that. Since the mass triaging in Africa during the last Water Crisis Africans had more or less disappeared, apart from those who'd got out when they could. Africa was empty, except for mining operations. Who cared about Africa?

Even lower down the pecking order was Social and Recreational. No-one cared much what they had to say— Burk knew that from experience. Burk had even had bosses who weren't Guardians, a sure sign that no-one took what they were doing seriously.

No-one listened to the junior ministers responsible for SurPops and AdPops—why should they?—and the

Department of the Environment took their cue from Industrial Development, conveniently housed in the building next door, if they knew what was good for them.

But Crime and Security? You didn't mess with them, unless you had a *very* good reason!

They might not be as sinister as Ideology, but they were everywhere, and you couldn't avoid dealing with them at some stage. They might treat ordinary citizens with ruthless, inflexible directness, but with the powerful they cut lots of deals in "sensitive" matters. (Pedophilia charges would never be brought against a senior Guardian, for instance.) The Minister could always call in favors if she was challenged.

Burk's spirits, which had plunged into the very depths of despair, now bounced happily back to the surface. He would live to fight another day, it seemed!

Guardian Rebek'a said nothing. Then, with a contemptuous grunt, and a furious glance at Burk that resonated with "You haven't heard the last of this", she tossed the communicator back to her colleague, turned on her heel, and walked out.

Her entourage followed her. As they left, some of the Crime and Security Guardians whispered mocking comments, before Guardian Sousanna silenced them with a fierce "Shush!"

There was no need to provoke her further. Guardian Rebek'a was already angry enough, and wounded predators are particularly dangerous.

CHAPTER SEVEN

BURK UNBOUND...AND ON THE LOOSE

Burk was a free man. Guardian Sousanna was as good as her word—the pedophilia charges were dropped. The charge of impersonating someone of higher status wasn't, but it was suspended, and would remain so ("providing you behave, of course").

He could leave whenever he liked. Burk still had a small living unit that he could go to—though he imagined that they'd probably ransacked it, looking for state secrets or for *sqot*—and he could once again start drawing the basic living allowance that he was entitled to as a lowly AdPop.

It was barely enough to survive on, but Burk had never deliberately resisted working. For AdPops, employment was seen as a privilege, a way of financing those little extras and luxuries that made life worth living; and it gave you personal dignity, he liked to think.

SurPops, on the other hand, avoided work like an infectious disease, and if they ran short—which did tend to happen, as the SurPop allowance was a very modest one—they could always supplement their income with pretty crime. Or with prostitution.

SurPops weren't always very attractive physically. In fact, they seldom were. But not every horny customer could afford to buy a session with a pleasure android, and some who *could* afford to preferred to "do it" with a real person, even with a dirty, dangerous SurPop. What was it that old Oscar Wilde had said about slumming it with rough trade: that it was like feasting with panthers? The danger was half the kick.

Not that there was much personal dignity in the Social and Recreational jobs that Burk had had so far: there were temporary, part-time contracts, with lots of dull admin, old ladies to talk to, and outings and club evenings to organize. But he'd look for work. Maybe Guardian Silvia could help.

He was given a new personal communicator, with which he could access his Life Account. He found that the basic living allowance had already been uploaded, and that he was again eligible to receive rations ("AdPop quality, DELICIO or comparable brands, plus bonus and fresh items in small quantities and as available"). Good. He wouldn't starve. His account information had been updated, and he was listed as living in his former quarters once again, meaning that the communicator would allow him entry.

He had even been given some credits for local transportation. This would cover his return to his living unit, and allow him to make a few other short trips. After that, he wouldn't be mobile until he found work (which would entitle him to generous transportation credits). The other option was to pay for a private transporter—which was out of the question. Or he could walk.

Walking was not really an option in the WAM, unless you had a death-wish. It wasn't just the traffic. True, the thoroughfares buzzed chaotically with official Guardian vehicles and private UsePop transporters, none of whose drivers seemed to know what they were doing. Or to care.

Theoretically, the transporters could be programmed with navigation software and driven automatically, but the control network had collapsed a century ago under the sheer weight of data, and since then people hadn't bothered, preferring instead to hurtle crazily around, past and sometimes into each other. The big, slow public transporters were actually the safest way to travel: because of their size, no-one wanted to collide with one of *them*. And you made sure not to smash into the luxury transporter of some high-ranking Guardian, for quite different reasons. Dental repairs, for instance, were expensive.

It wasn't just the traffic, though. It was also the monstrous pollution, which made any outdoor activity a serious health hazard. On top of which, you could barely see where you were walking anyway, unless you programmed your communicator to navigate for you (and since every big urban sprawl was an uncontrollable mess of building and rebuilding, of renaming and renumbering, few bothered even to try).

Because of the upcoming enquiry, Burk had to stay in the WAM. It was the center of world government, and had been ever since the cities of the Eastern American Megalopolis had been overwhelmed by a huge tsunami caused by the eruption of Pico del Teide on Tenerife. Some of the urban formations of the EAM had been reconstructed, and people still lived there, but the area had never recovered its significance. The EAMies had once made jokes about their western cousins squatting on top of a giant earthquake waiting to happen, but it was their own catastrophe that had arrived first.

The WAM was where Burk lived, and where most of his employment had been, but given a choice he would rather have taken a break and gone to Old Europe. Back in the twentieth-first century the ageing population there had been in decline. The demographic slide was halted by an influx of labor from outside Europe, especially from areas which had failed to modernize and which were going bankrupt as fossil fuels were phased out. Yet while the mass immigration had rescued the local economies it had also caused social unrest. Meanwhile, other parts of Europe were in a desperate condition, scorched by the final flare-up with Russia.

Terra had had a world government for so long now that it felt strange looking back at those old squabbles between petty nation states. A bit like getting out a box of toy soldiers in funny uniforms and setting them up to fight each other, without being quite sure which countries they were supposed to represent.

Europe had settled down long ago. The populations had intermarried; religion, the cause of much of the conflict, had almost died out (except as a curiosity, cultivated by eccentric enthusiasts); and the whole place was like one giant museum. This was the big attraction for Burk. It was so quaint, and there were so many old things to look at. There were fleamarkets where you could buy old-fashioned books printed on paper, and some people had small *kitchens* in their homes, with antiquated cooking devices, and actually prepared all their own food! His work had occasionally taken him to Europe, and he would have loved to go there again.

But Burk couldn't go. Even if there hadn't been the enquiry, there was no way he could pay for the rapid transportation to get him there. And then there was Milliya—she was somewhere out there in the WAM, and he needed to know what had happened to her.

Before he left the Terminal, Guardian Sousanna told him that he would be watched.

"For your own good. A Guardian sentry on her own outside your living unit won't stop Rebek'a's thugs from snatching you. We can't give you that protection. But a girl posted conspicuously outside your living unit will tell them that *we don't want you snatched*, that we'll know if they do it, and that there'll be consequences. I think they'll leave you alone. It's not *you* that they're really after, is it?"

No, it was Milliya. And that was the real reason why one of Guardian Sousanna's team would be posted there: not to look after *him*, but to be on the lookout for *her*. But he didn't say any of that.

He found that his living unit had indeed been ransacked. It was an unattractive little capsule to start with—what an AdPop, Lower Executive Level, was entitled to, no more and no less—and now it looked even worse.

He was hungry, but there were no rations in the tiny food storage and preparation area. Had they been looted? Were Guardian rations so crappy that they had to steal his miserable DELICIO junk? Or had they just chucked it out? There was no cause for that: rations could be stored for an eternity, and though he'd been to Lemnos, light years distant in the Zora system, and back again, in real time it was as if he'd been on a holiday trip. That particular problem had held space travel back for half a century or more. Now it took only a few metabolic adjustments, carried out while you were being "frozen" and "defrozen" in the transportation pods, and you hardly felt that you'd been away.

He needed to get out. He wanted some proper food, and he wanted to look for Milliya. In both cases that meant going downtown

Sure enough, there was a Guardian in a transporter posted outside. She wasn't one that he recognized—some young trainee, perhaps?—but he was reasonably confident that he could fool her (with Guardian Anfea he wouldn't have been so sure).

There was a small lobby at the back of the block of living units, seldom used but clogged with all the equipment of the cleaners and with cartons and boxes waiting for recycling. Hidden behind the piled-up garbage and the crates containing pressure hoses and paint spreadguns was a door, which had been installed fairly recently to make it easier to move those items in and out of the building without having to lug them all the way to the front entrance.

Guardian Anfea would have checked the entrances and exits on her own initiative, even without having been instructed to, and she would have done it on foot; the trainee had doubtless preferred to stay warm and dry in her transporter, and check the details of the building on her comunicator. But the information on the communicator was only as accurate as the last update had made it—and who had time to worry about that kind of stuff? Certainly not López, their indolent janitor.

Burk had cultivated the amiable AdPop, winning his favor by showing him how to get the most out of his entertainment center, sensory effects and all, at the cost of having to listen to López recounting how he'd "nailed" that Gloriya, in every way you could imagine and some you couldn't—cybersexually, naturally. (Burk would one day get some fun out of telling him how Gloriya had tried to rape him on board the *Starstretcher*, and about the things he'd seen at her swinger party on Lemnos.) He'd also helped López to manipulate some of his reports, and done the tiresome monthly updates for him.

"That's what we learn in Media Studies, and I'm grateful to have the chance to practice. I need to keep my hand in!"

Which is how he knew that the backdoor entrance was not on anybody's screen. López had also given him the code for the door, so that Milliya could slip into and out of the building unobserved.

Burk was illicitly shagging a Guardian! That impressed the janitor deeply, and he was happy to be of assistance. He would leer knowingly, and with his fingers make gestures suggestive of penetration. "Amor, Señor!" Many of the AdPops and SurPops in the WAM still used Spanish among themselves.

Leaving the building was therefore the easy part. Getting a ride downtown was more complicated. If he called for a private transporter, using his communicator, the Guardians would know it immediately; he also doubted that he had enough credits for that. If he booked a public transporter to collect him from the nearest pickup point, they might notice that too.

The solution was to go to the pickup point and find a good-natured passenger waiting to travel downtown; then to ask them to take him with them on their ride as a "dependant family member". No name would need to be keyed in. In return, he would transfer some transportation credits from his own communicator to theirs, to be used at a later date. An incriminating code-number would eventually flash up on the screen in front of some Guardian controler, but that could be days away...

An obese, elderly UsePop, struggling with several shopping containers, was willing to oblige in return for help with his heavy load. It consisted of old-fashioned downloads of movies, the kind of raunchy material that you might not want to keep around the house on a device. The UsePop's wife had discovered his stash of treasures, and demanded that they be disposed of, but she was too mean to just throw them out. Instead, her husband should take them downtown and sell them. There were specialist merchants there for anything, literally anything, which you had to offer.

By the way, was Burk himself interested…? No, Burk was only interested in the ride. But he escorted the man to the address that he showed him.

It was the sort of area where Guardians patroled in teams—if they dared to patrol at all. The smog was dense. You couldn't see far ahead, and walking was dangerous because of the ruts and chasms in the sidewalk. House entrances stank of urine, or drugs. Pale, unfriendly faces peered at them from doorways and windows: SurPop addicts, prostitutes, thieves, runaways, dealers. No-one respectable chose to live in this part of town.

Burk had a strong feeling that they were being followed.

If they *were* stopped by Guardians, there might be difficulties, depending on exactly what was in the containers. Porn was no problem. Drugs might be—because the Government had a monopoly, and objected to freelance dealers. Worst would be if Jolyon had any subversive material hidden in the containers.

Jolyon didn't look like a Ciaranite; if anything, he looked like an older, overweight version of Aylwin, the settler on Lemnos (or what Aylwin would finally look like when his lifestyle and dirty habits caught up with him). Jolyon: what sort of name was that? It was British, Jolyon told him proudly, and had been in his family for half a millennium.

They found the dealer in dirty movies, though not before Burk had tripped several times and Jolyon had fallen flat on his face in a dirty gully. As he got up, he said that a rat had scampered over him. Burk didn't care, and was happy to leave Jolyon and his containers at the emporium of a sleazy-looking AdPop named Keyzer ("Just call me 'The Source'"). He and Jolyon seemed to be old friends.

In response to his request, the dealer gave Burk a few addresses where he could obtain some fresh food, and might perhaps also find runaways and fugitives. Burk's hope was that Milliya had been able to give her captors the slip and had gone underground; or, if she was cooperating with the Ciaranites, that they had left her in a safe lodging somewhere.

He wasn't going to try and fight it out with the Ciaranites to rescue Milliya, nor was he going to ask people in this part of town whether they knew anywhere that Ciaranites hung out: the first local inhabitant with a communicator that he asked would betray him to the Guardians for the reward money.

As he was leaving, the dealer asked Burk whether he was armed.

"Of course not. I'm a Recreational Officer!"

Would he like to purchase a taser? Or something cheaper, but equally effective? The streets were not safe. No? A pity.

Burk was inclined to agree with him, and was already wondering how he was going to get back. He'd need to find a transportation pickup point and repeat his trick, and it wouldn't be so easy to find someone traveling away from downtown and in his direction.

First, though, he must check out the addresses.

The Source had keyed them into Burk's communicator, but the navigation function refused to recognize them. He'd have to ask some of the people lurking in doorways and staring at him ominously as he walked past. He'd been hoping to avoid that.

Before he could try his luck with the locals, something hard poked into his back and a gruff female voice said, "Walk on, AdPop, to the end of this street, and go through the archway. Don't talk, and don't turn round."

Oh no: a Guardian! What was he going to do now?

He sensed that it was only one person, and not a patrol.

"Please, Guardian, I'm on my way home. I won't trouble you at all."

"Shut up and keep walking."

The voice was troublingly familiar. Could it be one of the Guardians from the Terminal?

At the end of the street was a ruined building without a roof. It could be entered through an ornate archway, in front of which was a foul-smelling gutter full of garbage and the remains of the door. Burk stepped across the gutter and entered the dark ruin.

"Now you can turn round, Burk, but keep your voice down. Don't you recognize me?"

It was Milliya's sister, Jeine. He wasn't sure whether to be relieved or not.

CHAPTER EIGHT

ENCOUNTER IN THE DARKNESS

Jeine wasn't fond of him. When her sister had told her that she was involved with an AdPop, Guardian Jeine Jahangiri had been horrified. And when they all met up once, briefly and discreetly, she hadn't been impressed by Burk.

She had told Milliya that she was a fool, and Burk that he was a crapulous waste of space, and then she let them get on with it. If her sister wanted to play dangerous games, she wasn't going to be the one who informed on her.

Milliya later mollified Burk (or tried to) by telling him that her sister much preferred him to Guardian Rebek'a, who was a thoroughly nasty piece of work. Burk, on the other hand, was merely...well, she wasn't going to repeat what Jeine had said, because it wasn't true.

Despite the darkness, Burk could see that Jeine wasn't wearing a conventional uniform, although she was a Guardian. But the way she was glaring at him, her eyes flashing angrily, was typical Guardian—he could see that even in the gloom of the ruined building. All that was missing was a taser pointed at his chest.

Jeine Jahangiri wasn't entitled to carry a taser. She had always been the brainy, academic one. She had studied, passed her exams, and gone into Science, and she was already a Grade II, on the brink of further promotion. Her normal Guardian uniform was probably protective lab clothing. It wasn't one of her duties to apprehend suspicious-looking AdPops out on the roam, though any responsible-minded Guardian might feel called upon to do so, in the absence of more robust colleagues from Crime and Security.

Now she wanted to know what Burk was doing downtown, prowling about and talking to lowlifes?

He told her the truth, that he was searching for Milliya (omitting to mention the bit about the food).

"And what a lovely coincidence, Jeine, meeting you here!"

"Don't be stupid, Burk. I've been tracking you, of course."

It had been easy for her to obtain his address, and she had been observing the living unit. She had spotted the Guardian watchdog immediately, and quickly formed her own opinion of her ("Pathetic! She deserves a thrashing. Or was she *told* not to do her job properly?"). Nor did it take her long to work out how many entrances there were. She had seen Burk sneak out, and followed him downtown.

Why hadn't she intercepted him straight away?

"Because I was curious to know what you were up to, Burk. But I would have spoken to you eventually. You're looking for my sister? Well, I have a message from her!"

If there had been anything to sit on, Burk would have sat down. He was trembling with excitement.

"Where is she?"

Jeine didn't know. Her sister had come to her lab, cleverly disguised as a cleaning contractor and with a fake identity. (Another one! Burk said to himself. The list of charges against her kept growing.) Whoever she was with, they were obviously not keeping her prisoner.

Burk was about to mention the Ciaranites, then thought better of it. Jeine might be clever—but she was also a straightforward Guardian, loyal to the Government, and with none of her sister's depths and shadows. She would have no sympathy with radicals or terrorists.

So what *was* Milliya doing?

"She said that they thought you were dead—those people she's with—but then they found out that you weren't. She told them not to worry, and that you would keep your mouth shut about it. I don't understand any of that. In any case, when did *you* ever keep your mouth shut?"

"There was a misunderstanding, in the course of which we were separated…"

Jeine snorted with contempt.

"Not permanently—unfortunately! She said that there would be an enquiry about Lemnos. She had useful information, she said, but it would be very difficult for her to attend. Very dangerous. *You* could be there, though, as a witness. 'Do whatever they tell you,' she said. 'Say whatever they want you to say. Don't fight. Don't resist. Survive. *And forget me.*' Those were her words."

"And that was all she said?"

"That was all. Quite a rigmarole, don't you think? If I thought you were leading her into danger, Burk, I would burn off every protuberant part of your body with concentrated Lemnian acid, and sell the rest to the Delicio Corporation. But it's the other way round, isn't it? I don't think you're bright enough to lead a complicated life without her help. And my little sister: *she* was always the complicated one." She paused. "You love her, don't you?"

"Yes, very much."

He hoped that she couldn't see that he had tears in his eyes. Tears of relief, but they were also tears of frustration. Did tears glow in the dark?

"Then that's good enough for me. Do what she says, Burk, if you understand what she means, that is—because I don't. Count me out of it, though. I have a Guardian career to worry about, and a family. But I'll bring you back to your living unit. My transporter is only two blocks away. This way."

She turned to lead him back out through the doorway. A rat scampered past them. Burk thought he heard a footfall.

"Did you hear that?"

"Don't spook me, Burk. It's late. I'm tired. I had a long day in the lab. There's no-one here."

He heard the sound again, out of the darkness. She wouldn't hear it, she was a Science Guardian, not Crime and Security. She wasn't trained like her sister. And she wouldn't be armed, either.

"Jeine, let's go the other way," he whispered.

It was already too late. They were surrounded.

In the darkness, he couldn't be sure how many of them there were. He saw the shapes of four of them; perhaps there were others standing behind them, holding back. But he heard them clearly enough.

"Hello, lover boy. You picked a bad, bad place for a shag. This is not going to be your night."

A strong, deep voice. Confident. Well-spoken. Maybe he'd once been an AdPop. The leader of the pack?

Then a second voice, more primitive, the typical Sur-Pop whine: "Yeah. Dirty, cold, wet. And we're gonna take your girl!"

And then there was some malevolent chuckling from further back. There were four of them altogether, he calculated.

Jeine snapped at them, "I'm a Guardian, on official business. Go now, while you have the chance!"

She sounded confident too, though Burk couldn't understand why. She wouldn't be carrying a taser, and they didn't train Science Guardians to kill with their bare hands. He had a distinctly sinking feeling in his stomach, and it wasn't because he was hungry.

The gang found her defiance very funny.

"Hey, a Guardian! Whatever next? Any of you ever screw a Guardian? Who wants to go first? Octopus?"

"Yeah, why not?"

Octopus was the SurPop with the whining voice. The other two disagreed.

"Why him?"

"He had the old woman in the shelter. Last night. I heard them! Why should he go first?"

"No, my boy Octopus goes first." The gang leader laughed nastily. "You know what they say about Guardians, don't you? They're all lezzies, and they've got sharp, pointed teeth down there, and not a little juice-box like other women. If she *has* got something nasty in her pants, let him be the one who finds out! You OK with that, Octopus?"

"I'm OK with that, Boss Man. They can hold her legs open. Don't worry, boys, I'll be quick the first time. Then *you* can play with her for a bit."

"Good man. And we don't need lover boy here, do we? Let me just deal with him, and then we can party!"

Burk shrank together, anticipating a blow, but it was Jeine who struck first. There was a gentle "Pop!", like the sound of a toy gun, as she shot something at the Boss Man's face. He screamed horrifically, and then he was lying on the ground at Burk's feet, writhing and screeching.

"One down, three to go! You don't mess with Guardians."

But the other three SurPops had already pulled back.

"Fuck, she *has* got a taser!"

"Kill the bitch!"

None of them tried to, though.

Suddenly there was light. Jeine had switched on a tiny wide-angle torch. The three SurPops now looked far less threatening than they had sounded: they looked like rats, Burk thought, and they were cowering together in shock. The one they called Octopus was bigger than the other two, but trapped in the torchlight none of them looked as if he wanted to take his chance with Jeine.

Then she flipped the torch downwards to illuminate the Boss Man as well, and Burk got a shock. The man was twitching and shaking, and blood was flowing out of his nose and welling up in his half-open mouth. His face was glowing in the torchlight, but he seemed to be sweating *blood*.

"Take a good look at him, you scum. He is losing blood from every orifice, and he has one hour to live. One hour maximum, unless you get him to a clinic. Just tell them 'Ebola'—they'll have the antidote. Pick him up, and take him there. Now! Or would you like the same treatment? Who wants to be zapped next? Two down means at least one dead, because you won't be able to carry them both, and *we're* not gonna help."

The SurPops picked up their leader and hurried him out through the doorway with surprising speed.

"I rather enjoyed that, Burk!"

"Won't they just dump him at the next corner and run? Or fetch weapons and come back?"

"No, I don't think they will. In that gang, he's the one with the brains, the imagination, and the contacts. Without him, they'll be lost."

"What *was* that? A new sort of taser?"

No, she said, she wasn't allowed to carry a taser. But she was a scientist, and she had access to other, more advanced weapons.

"Including this dandy little item." She held out what looked to Burk like a small, old-fashioned pistol, before slipping it into her pocket. "It fires interesting pellets. Today it was loaded with hemorrhagic fever, very unpleasant indeed."

"I've never heard of it."

"Why should you have? There were different sorts, you know. They used to ravage western Africa, until we eradicated them in the twenty-first century. Except that we *didn't* eradicate them—we kept them in the laboratory; we tinkered with them; and we weaponized them. They're not infectious, but they're deadly, unless you get treated at once."

She explained that the guns had been perfected just as world government was being set up. Conventional wars unfortunately came to an end!

"Sad: all that work, all that research, and the guns end up locked away in a cupboard. Then again, tasers are *so* much more suitable for police and security work.

They're easier to use; they have all those useful settings; and they're not so dangerous to handle as these things are."

"But you said they weren't infectious?"

"Did I say that? It was the intention, though they never completed the clinical trials. But those SurPops will be alright, I guess."

"And the one they called Boss Man? Won't he die?"

"If the boys are polite to her, the doctor might order an antidote by supply chute. Discreetly. They won't have one there in the clinic. These fevers no longer exist, remember? An hour, though—that'll be cutting it very fine. Still, I ask you, is that *our* problem?"

"I suppose not."

But Jeine's remarks had put a chill on the conversation.

"Come on, man, be thankful that I had the gun with me. I wasn't going to go out hunting for you without *some* kind of weapon, was I now? And on the spur of the moment I couldn't think of anything more effective to take along with me than this little old darling." She tapped the gun in her pocket. "Good to give it a spin now and again."

They made their way to Jeine's transporter, and she brought him back to his living unit, where he slipped in by the same door that he had used to slip out.

The trainee Guardian was still posted outside, unaware that he'd ever been gone.

CHAPTER NINE

BURK RECEIVES FIRST ONE INVITATION, AND THEN ANOTHER ONE

Time passed slowly. Burk had no job, and his basic allowance didn't allow him to get out much. He therefore spent long hours plugged in to the entertainment center, but the movies were dreadful, with or without the sensory effects, and he soon tired of Government productions about space exploration and the bringing of Terran civilization to distant star systems.

They made it sound so glorious: after eons of emptiness and meaninglessness the universe had at last found its fulfillment thanks to the human species.

He'd been to Lemnos; and he knew that there was a dark side that would never be shown in the documentaries.

The upcoming public enquiry that had been announced—"into the conditions on Lemnos"—at least hinted that not everything was perfect. But it wouldn't really be public: attendance would be by invitation only, and while the event was being held under the auspices of the Imperial Advisory Council, media coverage would be controled by the Government.

They would cancel each other out! Burk thought to himself.

His invitation to appear as a witness didn't come. He wasn't surprised. Why should the Government bother to call an AdPop as a witness, if they believed that the Council had Milliya in its power? Or had simply disposed of Milliya, and her evidence? Burk's testimony on its own, and without the recordings, would be worthless anyway. He had no illusions about his own unimportance in the greater scheme of things. That had been made abundantly clear to him. As far as everyone was concerned, he was "surplus to requirements".

Milliya wouldn't be at the enquiry. How could the Ciaranites smuggle her in, even if they wanted to? They had taken her, but how were they going to use her? Would they want to ally themselves with *either* party? They might even choose to let the Council do their dirty work for them, embarrassing and compromising the Government.

Why had Milliya sent him the message to "do what they told him"? But also to "say whatever he wanted to say"? Wasn't that a contradiction? And who was meant by "they"? The Government was showing no interest in him. Only Guardian Rebek'a would definitely want to see him again, and what *that* might entail was a train of thought that he didn't want to pursue.

Milliya appeared frequently in his dreams; Guardian Rebek'a loomed up in his nightmares.

The weeks passed, the date of the enquiry grew nearer, and Burk felt helpless, and increasingly depressed. But then something occurred that cheered him up considerably.

He had sent Guardian Silvia a message, to which at first there was no reply. The retired Grade III Guardian had always helped him, even mothered him, in the past, and the old lady, although she no longer had any great influence, was universally respected. He had hoped that she might be able to organize a temporary or part-time job for him.

Then she rang him. It wasn't a text message, but a proper voice-call. A personal voice-call, from a senior Guardian to an unemployed AdPop—that was quite an honor!

She commiserated with him over his problems. She explained that there were no vacancies that she could recommend him for, though she wouldn't give up on him, and she was confident that something suitable might soon come along. She would keep on looking.

Then she told him about the enquiry. To her great surprise, she had been appointed as a judicial assessor.

Judicial assessors—there were normally two of them—assisted the judge (or, in this case, the person presiding over the enquiry) in an advisory capacity. Assessors couldn't overrule or outvote the Chairperson on any point of law, but their advice, especially if it was ignored, could play a role if the case went to appeal.

They were people of wide experience and known integrity—retired senior Guardians, for instance—but they were not required to be judges or lawyers, even though in practice they often had a legal background or training. Burk knew that Guardian Silvia had studied Law at university, before she became an administrator in Social and Recreational.

As an assessor, she was entitled to invite a few friends and colleagues to attend. ("Friends"—that sounded good! Burk had almost got to the point where he thought he no longer had any.) As a retired person, Guardian Silvia had only a limited number of social contacts. (Burk dared to contradict her, but she would have none of it: "No, I'm an old lady, and I don't go out much.") She knew that Burk had just been to Lemnos—would he be interested in attending the enquiry? If so, she would send an invitation to his communicator. And they must also get together for tea and cookies sometime, when he could tell her all about his adventures, though not until after the enquiry of course.

Yes, he would be delighted! And the invitation to attend the first day of the enquiry promptly arrived on his communicator.

So he would be there after all. Not as a witness, but then why had he ever expected to be taken seriously? He was only an AdPop. It would be an interesting experience, and afterwards he would hope to find some kind of work. If Guardian Silvia couldn't help him, there were less attractive assignments that he could apply for where even he, with his blotchy personnel record, might stand a chance.

As a Recreational Officer at one of the great environmental rejuvenation projects in China, say? Back in the previous century, unimaginable pollution levels had forced three-quarters of the population there to be evacuated. The boys who were now cleaning up the muck needed to be entertained! (Not the SurPop convicts, naturally, but their Guardian watchdogs, and the clerical staff, and the teams of scientists.)

Burk began to surf through the announcements of Situations Vacant on Terra. Nothing further afield. He had no wish to return to Lemnos, even if they allowed him to, and the other planetary settlements were mostly grim mining stations, prisons, waste recycling facilities and the like. These paid well, but they were bearable only if you had a top job, with lots of privileges.

Late on the afternoon of the day before the opening of the enquiry, Burk had an unexpected visitor. The gentleman didn't announce himself at the door: he was suddenly there, in the living unit, standing perfectly still and looking at Burk. He looked at Burk as though he was something that had been through the digestive system of his mother-in-law. The man was a Grade II Guardian, but wearing a uniform that Burk had only ever seen on a monitor, and never in reality and close-up: the smart uniform of the Imperial Guard.

Burk was paralyzed with surprise. The Guardsman was very big, and radiated an aura of repressed violence. Repressed viciousness, even.

"You're the AdPop John Burk? Please confirm your identity." And, when Burk at first failed to respond: "It's rude to stare. And unwise to waste my time."

"Sorry."

Burk handed him his personal communicator, after he had quickly tuned it to his account details.

The Guardsman checked the information on the display, nodded, and gave the communicator back to him.

"You don't need to know who I am. I'm only here to collect you. Someone at the Palace wants to meet you. Have you ever been to the Palace?"

"No."

"I hardly thought you had! Take a shower, change into something cleaner, and then leave this building by your favorite route. Oh yes, we know all about you, Burk: you and your tricks! Once you're out on the street, turn right, and follow it for two hundred meters or so. Then turn left into the alleyway where a delivery chute repair transporter is always parked. My own vehicle is parked just behind it. Don't leave any messages. Don't contact anyone to say where you're going. We'll find out if you do, and we won't be pleased! And make sure no-one follows you. We know you're good at that. Native cunning, perhaps? Or did your treacherous little girlfriend train you? Be there in thirty minutes. If you aren't, I'll come looking for you. Believe me, you won't want *that* to happen!"

And then he was gone.

CHAPTER TEN

A WALK THROUGH A GARDEN FULL OF BIRDS AND BUTTERFLIES, WITH AN ASCENT TO A MEETING IN THE SKY

If Burk had expected to be taken in through the majestic front entrance of the Imperial Palace, he was soon disappointed. His Guardsman escort plainly intended that they should not be seen. That was clear from the roundabout route to the Palace that they took, through dirty backstreets and lanes, and the way that the Guardsman darkened the windows of the transporter as soon as Burk had found his seat.

Also, unusually, the Guardsman was alone. He was on a confidential mission—the fewer the people who knew about it, the better.

Burk sat back in the comfortable seat. It was upholstered in soft leather—*real* leather, surely? He stroked it, enjoying the unfamiliar feeling, which was quite unlike that of the synthetic materials that he was used to. The upholstery was decorated with the Imperial monogram, a crowned "17." Emperors had no names; they lost them when they acceded to the title. Since there was only one Emperor at any one time, the ruler didn't need a personal name, because there could never be any confusion of identity. For formal and titular purposes, however,

Emperors were known by their number. The current one was "The Seventeenth".

By an ancient agreement, Emperors were elected in rotation, from the main power blocs that had dissolved themselves to end the era of nation states and begin the Era of Terran Unity. The Seventeenth was elderly, and colorless (at least that was the impression that Burk had always had). He was from the North American bloc, and had grown up not far away from the Western American Megalopolis. His predecessor, who had been kept alive until He was 140, had been from the area formerly known as Japan.

They drove round to the undistinguished back of the Palace, where the service entrances were. The Guardsman opened a sliding door by remote control, and the transporter glided down a long ramp into the dark bowels of the building, before coming to a halt in a gloomy underground parking lot that was half full of official vehicles.

"Get out, follow me, and keep your mouth shut."

Was he being taken to some sinister dungeon to be interrogated? Probably not. He hadn't been manacled, or tasered. He wasn't blindfolded either. And the unfriendly tone of voice of the Guardsman was nothing unusual—AdPops were used to being talked to like that. It could be normal conversation. Or it could be the prelude to a savage beating. You never knew.

They walked for some distance down silent, murky corridors. Burk was just beginning to grow accustomed to the darkness when they turned a corner and the corridor transformed itself into a long, slow-moving travelator that curved up ahead of them towards a bright light high in the distance.

At the top of the travelator they found themselves in an immense covered hall, filled with trees, flowers, artificial lakes, and water-courses. Birds fluttered and twittered above their heads. Real birds? Burk saw butterflies, too, in many different colors. Then he felt spots of wetness on his face: they were standing next to a row of sprinklers, and he was being splashed.

This was the famous Green Dome, the Emperor's private garden, where His Imperial Majesty would seek recreation and distraction from His arduous constitutional duties (or so the commentary on documentaries about the Imperial Palace).

The Guardsman suddenly pulled Burk towards him and hissed, "Do *exactly* what I do!"

A party of important people was approaching, preceded by and flanked by a detail of Imperial Guardsmen. As they came nearer, Burk saw that what this substantial bodyguard was protecting was no more than a gaggle of expensively- and foppishly-dressed courtiers.

His own Guardsman escort stepped back and made a slow, dignified bow. Burk did his best to imitate him. As he looked up, two things struck him immediately.

The people in the group walking past them were rich, influential, possibly even dangerous...*and yet all of them were men!* How unusual that was. Burk had grown up in a world where it was generally women who had the say, who wielded the power, and who were able to make your life difficult or unpleasant as they wished.

Secondly, he saw how the courtiers all had their attention turned inwards, adjusting their pace to the needs of the oldest member of the group, who was dressed completely in white: the Emperor!

So *this* was the ruler of the entire known universe: an elderly, slightly hunched gentleman with an inane smile on His face and His hand moving unceasingly in greeting and benediction. The smile was bestowed on Burk, too, for a brief moment, catching him like the revolving beam of an old-fashioned lighthouse, and then the Imperial party had moved on.

He was not actually the *ruler* of anything at all, Burk knew, despite all the actions taken in His name. His job was to do what Burk had just seen: to smile, to be respected, and to be moved around like a doll. His duty was to give His assent—constantly. Had He ever *not* given it? Was the word "dissent" even in the man's vocabulary?

Did He have an identity of his own? What was His real name? Burk couldn't remember, though he had once known it, as a schoolboy, when he had loved learning by heart lists of obscure dynastic rulers or capital cities of nation states, all of them long gone, and had also memorized the titles, personal names and origins of the seventeen Emperors. Did the Emperor Himself remember His own name? He had no need to.

The Guardsman pushed Burk towards an open elevator, which propelled them smoothly up through the vegetation towards the ceiling of the Green Dome. Burk marveled at the colorful bird and insect life all around them. Where else could anything like this still be found on Terra? Perhaps in the few remaining tiny pockets of the Amazon rainforest (though rumor had it that these had now disappeared).

As the ceiling grew nearer, Burk saw that it was fashioned to resemble a transparent window to the blue sky outside. Of course, there *was* no blue sky outside, only murk and pollution, and what little daylight there was would be drawing to a close anyway now, but it was a clever illusion. Burk knew what a blue sky looked like from the movies that he watched on his entertainment center; even more strikingly so from the same movies when they were shown in public entertainment halls, with special 360 degree effects.

It was still a shock, however, when the elevator stopped at a landing just below the ceiling of the Dome, and the Guardsman led Burk through a sliding door and out onto the roof of the Palace.

The darkness! The Megalopolis stretched out for miles in every direction, its lights twinkling and flickering bravely into the early evening gloom like tiny assertions of human existence. But it was a hopeless cause—they had no real chance against the darkness. Once upon a time the natural light of Terra had been all but extinguished, by smog and gas and industrial muck, and it was now too late: the proper light that earlier generations of mankind had apparently known was never going to return.

They were on a sort of viewing platform, and the man that Burk had been brought here to meet was waiting for them. Burk recognized him at once.

He was smaller and older than Burk, and exquisitely (but tastefully) dressed. As he approached them, Burk, seeing him for the first time in real life, and not on a monitor or a screen, saw that he had beautiful, symmetrical features, like those of an android movie star, but without any touch of effeminacy. Burk had no sexual interest in men, but he had to admit that, physically at least, this was a remarkably attractive human being.

The Guardsman saluted him. Burk didn't know what to do or say—this man outranked by far any of the senior Guardians that Burk had encountered in his life—and to his own embarrassment all that he could produce was a pitiful "Hello, my name is Burk!"

He sensed the Guardsman behind him quiver with outrage. Oh dear, what had he done? How pathetic he was!

But the man smiled, and then laughed, quite pleasantly.

"Yes, I know who you are, Mr. Burk. I sent this gentleman to collect you." He turned to look at the Guardsman. "But you can go now, Stepharn. I'll send for you when I need you."

Guardsman Stepharn was not happy about this.

"Your Excellency, shouldn't I…?"

"No. I don't need a bodyguard. Why should I? I'm going to make Mr. Burk a very happy man. I'm going to make him an offer that he can't refuse. And besides, Mr. Burk doesn't know how many forms of martial art I've mastered in my free time, does he? Despite his size and weight, I could throw him—I could throw *both* of you—off this platform without any great difficulty. Now go, please."

He waited until the Guardsman had withdrawn before asking Burk if he happened to know who he was? Had the Guardsman perhaps intimated to him…?

"No, Your Excellency, but I've seen you many times in news reports, and documentaries. You're the Secretary to the Imperial Advisory Council, Stelios Dagon. Sorry, *Count* Stelios Dagon. Sorry, I'm not used to this."

Again the pleasant laughter.

"Oh, don't worry, Mr. Burk. Titles of nobility were abolished many centuries ago, and 'Count' is just part of my name, passed down within my family for generations, and not an aristocratic title. But I'm sure you know all that. You're a well-read man. We know all about your reading habits! Which I share, by the way. When we've put all this silly fuss and bother behind us, I'll be happy to show you my private library. *Real books*, made of paper, thousands of them. Some are leather-bound, would you believe? And some even have the author's signature. Those poets of yours, for instance…"

"Yes, sir, I'd like that very much."

"I know that!"

"But why have you brought me here, sir, and what do you want from me in return? I'm only an unemployed AdPop, a very insignificant person. I can't imagine how I could be of use to you."

The Count fixed him with his gaze. His eyes were bright and intelligent, but cold.

"Yes, you can, Mr. Burk. We both know that."

"No, I'm sorry—"

The Count interrupted him.

"Don't try to fool me, Mr. Burk. At this moment, I know *exactly* what you're thinking. And it's time for me to tell you something. In fact, I'm required by Terran law to tell you this: that I'm a telepath."

CHAPTER ELEVEN

BURK IS MADE AN OFFER HE CAN'T REFUSE

It was bad, but it could have been worse.

Telepaths were exceptionally rare, and those with 50% telepathic capacity or higher were kept in special closed units run by Ideology. Their gifts were exploited for spying and interrogation purposes. (And being wired up for sixteen hours a day wasn't much of a life.)

"Good that I'm only 30%," the Count said with a laugh, "or Rebek'a would have me on a leash like a sniffer-dog!"

But there were even less attractive fates for telepaths, he went on to say. When the phenomenon had first been discovered, genuine and imagined telepaths in many parts of Terra had been lynched or burnt as witches. It was therefore easy to pass a law that allowed them to be taken into custody "for their own protection". Mild telepaths were later released back into the community, but were legally obliged to announce their status at the beginning of any one-on-one interaction with a stranger. If they didn't, and the interaction ended with sex, it was counted as statutory rape.

Yes, it was bad, Burk thought, while the Count was still speaking, but it could have been worse.

Because telepaths couldn't "listen" and talk at the same time, at least not efficiently. Burk would have to encourage the Count to do the talking, while trying to keep his own mind a blank when he responded. And 30% would be patchy anyway. But how much had the Count already "heard"?

"Don't worry, Mr. Burk, I'm not desperately interested in reading your mind." He laughed again. "No offence intended—I'm sure your mind is very interesting! But what Rebek'a has told me is probably enough to be going on with. You asked me how you could be of use to us? I'll tell you: by giving testimony to the enquiry tomorrow, if you are called. Your testimony will be as follows: that the present Government has raped and exploited the planet of Lemnos, endangering the most intelligent alien life form so far discovered in the universe."

Burk spoke before the Count could read the thought that sprang immediately to his mind.

"But I saw the settlers—your allies—destroying *sqot*."

"Excellent, Mr. Burk, you're being open with me. Perhaps I don't even need to read your thoughts! So I'll be open with you. What you saw on Lemnos was indeed certain people, certain good friends of ours if you like, clearing the *sqot* and carrying away *sqot*-impregnated topsoil."

He paused, and Burk fell into the trap.

"Yes, you want to ask, and why should they do that? For this reason: because the enriched topsoil has an immense explosive charge, greater than anything so far discovered by our species. Forget those childish little radioactive bombs that the twentieth century got so excited about! Those were just toys in comparison. Unfortunately our scientists are still working on possible trigger mechanisms. No completely reliable solution has yet been found. Our experiments have been only partially successful.

There *were* explosions, but they were not as controlable as we would have wished. In absolute confidence: the conflagration that destroyed Greater Montevideo two years ago (you do remember that?) was not caused by a reactor explosion. It was just one of those...*partially successful experiments*. Since we know that *sqot* can control these forces, the solution will probably involve a trigger mechanism that includes gene-manipulated *sqot*. But if you have any idea of the genetic complexity of *sqot* you will understand the magnitude of the task that our scientists have undertaken. So we need more time."

"And you aren't trying to eradicate *sqot* completely?"

"Eventually, yes. You see, Mr. Burk, *sqot* is an evil green parasite, a curse. The curse of Lemnos! We should regret the day that we ever discovered Zora and its planets. We don't understand *sqot*, but my particular personal gift has made me aware that it has an agenda that is not compatible with that of the human race. If we ever lose control over it, if it ever gets loose... No, we are committed to destroying it utterly, except for the very small quantity that we need for our project, of course."

"And for eating!"

The Count was visibly amused.

"Ah, yes, a small amount has been reserved for *culinary* purposes. Dear Rebek'a introduced you to that rare delight, I believe? How does she put it?" He imitated her voice. "'It's like eating a kiss, or a scream. Or both at the same time.' She's always so melodramatic! Talking of food—and I'm not reading your mind, Mr. Burk—perhaps we should adjourn our talk for a short break? My staff has prepared a modest buffet supper for us. I imagine that some *sqot* could also be provided, if you would care to partake? No, I sense that you don't."

The Count led him further along the platform until they came to a security gate, where he placed his hand on a scanner. The gate slid open.

"Oh!"

Burk was genuinely impressed. This, the Count informed him, was the Imperial Viewing Platform. The air where they had previously stood was thick and disgusting, but here it was pure and sweet, an artificial atmosphere kept fresh by perfumed air-jets. There were several comfortable chairs, including a large one upholstered in white leather that was presumably the Imperial Throne.

"Yes, Burk, you *may* sit on it. Privileged tourists are often brought here, and they always ask that question. How boring! It's only a chair, after all. And His Imperial Majesty doesn't come here very often."

Burk perched gingerly on the throne for a few seconds, trying to suppress the thought that he was probably the first AdPop ever to sit on it. If the Count *did* read that thought, he didn't comment on it. Instead, he pointed to the food, which was laid out on a row of ornamental tables.

While the Count barely ate anything, Burk tucked in with relish—he didn't need to be asked twice. Everything was fresh, and made of Terran produce that ordinary citizens never encountered. The range of fresh fruits alone fascinated Burk. Most of them were familiar to him only from their mouth-watering images and descriptions on his information monitor. So *this* was what mangoes tasted like! And peaches! And what was *this one* called, a yellow fruit with a delightfully sweet but tart flavor and flesh that melted in your mouth?

There were also items from Lemnos, including Goro-nuts by the plateful and flasks of expensive Goro-nut whiskey.

No *sqot* was in evidence, and Burk was not going to ask for any.

After a few minutes, the Count put his half-empty plate to one side and said, "Time to talk business, Mr. Burk! What are we offering you, apart from this delicious buffet? I did say that we would make you an offer that you couldn't refuse, and so here is the package:

—First, and most important, we'll give you your own life (and I have to say that Rebek'a took some persuading on that particular score);

—Second, the traitor Milliya's life, too—if she is still alive, of course—but she will be stripped of her Guardian status, and banished;

—Third, you will be granted UsePop status, and we'll find you some useful and well-paid employment. Maybe something cultural? Or a university job?;

—And, finally, a small present, which is already waiting for you at your temporary quarters here at the Palace. Enjoy it tonight, and if you cooperate with us tomorrow the arrangement will be made permanent. I'm certain that you *will* like it. Interestingly, it was Rebek'a who made the suggestion, sure proof that she now no longer means you harm.

So: how's that for generosity? What has the Government offered you? Anything at all? Will they even keep you alive?"

"But in return you are asking me to lie for you."

"You don't think our package is attractive enough? Oh dear! Most people can be bought, as simple as that, but you, Mr. Burk...you obviously have a moral dimension, a *hungry conscience* that also needs to be fed! Don't forget that you may not even be called upon to testify, in which case what we are offering you—merely for your silence—is very generous indeed. And if your testimony is called for, then 'lie' is surely not the best word for what I would expect of you. I'm asking you simply to *overlook* certain things that you saw on Lemnos, and to confirm certain other things that you didn't see, but for which we shall provide convincing documentation."

Burk laughed. There was no point in trying to hide his thoughts from the Count—he needed an answer.

"You mean the fake evidence that we were given by the settlers on Lemnos?"

"Yes, that was our original intention: to have you collect material on Lemnos—carefully prepared material—to show that the Government had been stripping and destroying *sqot* on a huge scale. Think of the impact that such a disclosure would have. The horror! A crime against civilization! Massive outrage among the population! The Government consequently falls, and wiser leaders step forward to take control of the state. I myself could even hope to be invited to play some small role in the New Order. And if you help us, Burk, there is a place for you, too, not in the forefront admittedly, but a very comfortable position nevertheless."

"You're asking me to sell my soul!"

"Of course! I'm Mephistopheles, Satan, or whatever, and you're Dr. Faustus. I hope you appreciate the literary references—I know what you studied at college. Or I have an even better one: 'He took him to a very high place, and showed him the kingdoms of the world in all their glory, and said: "All these will I give you, if you will only fall down and do me homage.'" Do you recognize *that* quotation?"

He beamed at Burk with almost malicious enjoyment.

"It's a religious text, isn't it? Probably the old Jesus cult?"

"I'll send you a copy of the book, Mr. Burk. A paper copy. They're not rare. Many millions were once printed. It makes for excellent reading. And it's appropriate, wouldn't you say? Here we are in a very high place, and I'm showing you our beloved Western American Megalopolis spread out below us"—he gestured out into the darkness behind him—"and asking you to sell your soul! Asking you to ally yourself with the forces of wickedness, and help to sabotage a noble, freely elected Government."

"If you put it like that, yes: that is what you're doing."

"But isn't that making it too simple? There are no heroes or villains here, Mr. Burk, there are only competing forces that are battling for power. Ah, the Government! Yapping females, not a man amongst them except for that idiot they've put in charge of Africa. At the risk of spoiling my digestion, I need to tell you what those preening bitches have been up to. The Government is not committed to destroying *sqot*, as we are, in fact for years their agents have been stripping it on Lemnos and bringing the green filth to Terra, where they are factory-farming it in Africa. Half of Africa is empty. No-one goes there, except agents of the Government, and the plantations are underground, or roofed over, so that they don't show up green from space, as Lemnos once did. And why are they doing this? For pharmaceutical reasons. But the quantity of *sqot* that the Government has brought to Terra is a danger to the whole planet. You are a moral person, Mr. Burk?"

"I suppose so."

"Then consider this, please. *Our* aim is to make explosives of unmatchable power, for military purposes, naturally, but also for construction and building work, here and in space. *Their* aim is to enslave the population of Terra with drugs. So who are the heroes, and who are the villains? As I said, two rival forces battling for control. You are a moral person, but also a realist, Mr. Burk—you understand these things."

"Three forces, surely..."

He paused, his head spinning with thoughts, and the Count had him trapped.

"Ah, you are thinking of the Ciaranites, because you have reason to believe that Milliya is in their hands!"

"Yes, perhaps." (What did it matter now?)

"When Milliya disappeared, we assumed that she had been taken by Government agents, masquerading as those gentlemen popularly known as the Outsiders. Rebek'a was most indignant, and she had quite a spat with her Guardian colleague Sousanna over this. But our spies can't locate her in any of the Government safe houses or holding centers, and our spies are very good—so we must now assume that she is dead. If the Ciaranites had her, wouldn't they have publicized it?"

"I suppose so."

Burk desperately tried to block out all thoughts of Milliya—that he knew from her sister that she was still alive. And it seemed to work.

"Even if she's *not* dead, and she makes some desperate attempt to gatecrash the enquiry, we will find means to prevent her appearance physically, and to solve the

Milliya problem once and for all. One way or the other, she won't testify, and so your testimony suddenly becomes of interest—or so I have convinced my colleagues on the Council. You can imagine what some of them said: he's not a Guardian, he's only a *man*, and so on and so forth. But I have faith in you, Mr. Burk. And I reminded them that in part our great undertaking is about restoring men to their rightful place at the center of events. No offence to Rebek'a, of course—she is the exception that proves the rule." He sniggered—it was the first time he had laughed unpleasantly. "She is exceptional in so many ways! On which note, it is time for you to enjoy the present that she so lovingly chose for you." He looked at the communicator on his wrist. "I'll call my friend Stepharn to show you to your quarters. Tomorrow will be a long day."

CHAPTER TWELVE

BURK UNWRAPS HIS PRESENT

Stepharn unlocked the guest living unit. Burk saw immediately that it was larger, and more luxurious, than any accommodation he had ever stayed in before.

"Not the usual AdPop hovel, eh? Enjoy it. Enjoy your present, too. It's in the food preparation area. I'll come and collect you for the enquiry at 0800, so don't go to bed too late. Not that you will!"

He seemed to find that last thought amusing.

When he had left, Burk began exploring his new residence. The entrance hall was palatial, and the living area was larger than his whole AdPop living unit, and with an entertainment center that took his breath away. In front of the enormous screen was a state-of-the-art pleasure couch, fitted with numerous attachments and connections. He knew the purpose of some of them, but others were probably intended for sophisticated pleasures that he could only guess at.

So this was how the privileged status groups lived!

The hygienic area was magnificent, and so was the sleeping area. It contained a triple-size, liquid-filled bed, which would match itself automatically to the contours of its occupants' bodies as they slept. There was a control panel for adjusting the temperature, the light, and the air quality, and for providing ergonomic sound wallpaper to optimize sleep quality.

Burk knew all about these things from Globopedia rather than from personal experience, though in some of his Social and Recreational jobs he had had to arrange temporary accommodation for visiting Guardians, and he had allowed himself a quick peep inside their guest living units.

Finally, he walked into the food preparation area. Standing in front of a raised work surface and chopping and mixing fresh food was Miss Bee-sting: Trainee Guardian Jeena.

"Oh!"

This *was* a surprise. As Burk struggled to collect himself, she treated him to the sweetest of smiles.

"Yes, Mr. Burk, I am your present. I hope that you are not disappointed? I have been instructed to take care of you, and to make you happy in any way that I can. At the moment I am preparing your breakfast for tomorrow."

"Your name is Guardian Jeena?"

"Please call me Jeena. My status is not important. I'll call you John, if I may? You have already eaten, I believe, but may I prepare you a drink? Fresh fruit juice? Or would you prefer a Goro-nut whiskey?"

"A whiskey, please."

"Please go into the living area and make yourself comfortable. I'll bring you your drink. And when I've finished preparing the breakfast I'll come and sit with you."

She was as good as her word. When she brought him the whiskey, and then returned for a few moments to the food preparation area, Burk saw that she was not merely pretty. She was wearing an off-duty version of the Guardian uniform that Burk had often seen Milliya dressed in. It accentuated the figure, and he saw that Jeena had a lovely body, slim and athletic, with just the right combination of softness and muscle. And she was all his, if he wanted her! He couldn't believe his good fortune.

But there was a price he would have to pay. Did it matter? They were all greedy rats, the Government and the Imperial Advisory Council, exploiting and manipulating the Terran population—one was no better than the other.

And then there was Milliya. He had always thought that she was the loveliest woman in the universe, but this one was even more gorgeous. He would be betraying Milliya, but hadn't she tricked and used him, to help her lover Rebek'a? And wasn't she now running with the Ciaranites? Through her sister, she had told him to forget her. Well, he would!

Jeena came in and sat beside him. He had chosen to sit on a leather-upholstered sofa rather than on the pleasure couch (that might be for later!). She hadn't made herself a drink. When he pointed that out, she replied that it was only his needs that mattered. What would he like to do next?

The idea of having a Guardian sex-slave was very arousing. It was every male AdPop's masturbation fantasy. But Milliya had never been a sex-slave—she had always been in command, however much she tried to give him pleasure too. This was a different (and very unfamiliar) situation.

"Please tell me something about yourself. His Excellency said that you might be willing to stay with me for longer?"

"What I want doesn't matter, John. I've been instructed to make you happy, and I shall do my best. It was

Guardian Rebek'a who observed that you found me attractive, and who had the idea of me being offered to you as an inducement. I'm only a Trainee Guardian, but I've been trained well."

Milliya had once been a Trainee Guardian, too, but he couldn't imagine her talking like that. Under any circumstances!

"You're such a beautiful girl, Jeena—you must have a boyfriend? Perhaps one of your Guardian Trainers?"

"Yes, I have had sex with my Trainer. It was part of my training. But he is not my boyfriend. What would you like to do, John? Oral? Vaginal? Anal? Sado-masochism? Or shall we go on the pleasure couch together? Let me strip for you while you make up your mind."

With smooth movements, and without any indication of shyness or shame, she began to remove her clothes. With such a fantastic body, why should she feel any shame? When she was naked, she took his head in her hands and drew it down to her breasts, inviting him to kiss them.

They were of medium size, perfectly shaped and very firm. Damn the thought, but did she have implants, despite being so young?

He kissed and licked at her nipples, then moved his mouth downwards over her sweetly shaped navel and flat stomach to the pubic mound. She was a natural blonde, her hair trimmed neatly in the way that he most liked.

The gate of paradise was open, and moist. She wanted him! She wasn't just obeying orders. He nuzzled at the portal, to take in her aroma. Except that there wasn't any—there was no noticeable smell, although she was obviously eager for sex. That puzzled him. All women (except SurPops) used vaginal deodorants, and many used whole-body aroma suppressants, but in his experience there was no chemical that could totally overwhelm the natural scent of a woman who wanted to make love.

He bent to kiss the soft flesh of her inner thighs, as he loved to kiss Milliya's, but her thighs didn't give way as hers did, they were more firm and solid. Was she an athlete?

A horrible suspicion began to dawn on him.

He raised his head and looked Jeena in the eye. She returned his gaze without blinking.

"Have you decided what you would like to do, Burk? The pleasure couch is very well-equipped, if you have a special need that I am not aware of."

"Jeena, you are without doubt the most beautiful woman I have ever seen naked. No, the most beautiful woman that I have ever seen, full stop. You have lovely blonde curls." He paused. "But do you never toss them?"

At the Disembarkation Terminal, Miss Bee-sting had tossed her curls flirtatiously. Here at the Palace she hadn't done it once.

Jeena's expression, one of earnest lustfulness, her eyes half closed, the glorious bee-stung lips half open, simply froze.

"What do you mean, John? Toss them *where*? Toss them *how*? Do you mean toss them in the sense of a coquettish gesture of female vanity? I can do that if you wish."

Her answer confirmed his suspicion, but he needed to be absolutely sure.

"Jeena, how do you feel about being used like this? About being told to have sex with me, whether you want to or not? What are your feelings about Guardian Rebek'a?"

"I have a deep feeling of respect for her. She is a wise and powerful Guardian, whose instructions should always be obeyed."

"And if she asked you to have sex with a dog?"

"I would do it. Sex with dogs is a well-known deviant form of sexual intercourse."

"And with a donkey?"

"I would do it. Sex with donkeys is also reported as a deviant form of sexual intercourse."

"And with a transporter?"

She hesitated. No, she *paused*.

"I would do that too. Sex with transporters is not a known form of sexual intercourse, but there are records of transporters attracting the interest of fetishists. However, I would need instructions on how to go about having sex with a transporter."

"Jeena, please wait here for me. I'm just going to the hygienic area."

"Can I help you there in any way, John? Would you like a shower massage? Do you enjoy water sports? Can I give you an enema?"

"No, just stay here...please."

Burk got up and went to the hygienic area. He locked the door, sat on the toilet, and gasped.

He had nearly had sex with a robot! Jeena was a pleasure android, not a human being.

He had never seen one close up, and they were not part of his sexual fantasy life. They were fabulously expensive. Building and programming an android to resemble the real Jeena would have taken days, and cost a fortune. This showed how much Rebek'a and the Count wanted his cooperation! Had the real Jeena been unwilling to do the dirty job? Or maybe they couldn't rely on her to keep quiet about it afterwards? After all, they were trying to overthrow the Terran Government.

Androids could be made to resemble people, sure, but they weren't humans.

There had been a great panic in the twenty-first century about whether silicon-based forms of intelligence (robots) would drive out carbon-based ones (living creatures). But it never happened. Robots had to be programmed, and they could even be programmed to continue learning on the basis of that earlier programming. But they couldn't be programmed to think or act truly *creatively*, except in foreseeable directions.

Robots could be programmed to follow random choices in specific situations or at specific intervals, but blue sky thinking, freakish creativity, the wild stab of genius, the brilliant guess...all that was beyond them. And if they were programmed to make several random choices in succession their circuits tended to break down.

Android Jeena had been programmed to follow normal human behavior patterns, and to answer most sorts of questions (they had probably uploaded the whole of Globopedia into her). But robots were unable to lie, unless they were deliberately programmed to lie in answer to specific questions.

Nor could robots be reliably programmed to be quirky and individualistic, to talk facetiously, or to behave in the strange, unpredictable ways that lovers behaved towards each other—lovers who were soulmates, and not just partners in coitus.

Damn! Milliya had her place in his heart, and that place couldn't be taken by an android.

Burk was aroused, but he couldn't bring himself to have sex with a robot. Milliya was probably gone from his life, but the memory of what it had been like with her (even if she had been deceiving him) was still there. So was the knowledge of what such a relationship might be like, if he could find the right partner.

He would look for that person.

In the meantime: no robots! If the Count had offered him a dirty sleepover with the real Jeena, yes, be honest, he would have gone for it. She was probably a dull little creature who would prostitute herself to an AdPop if that was what her training required. (As Milliya had prostituted herself, too, he couldn't help thinking.) It would be just a shag, soon forgotten. Ah well, since the real Jeena wasn't available, he'd have to use his hand. Then he'd go back into the living area, tell Android Jeena that he had a headache, and suggest that they go to bed. He wouldn't confront her—*it*—with his discovery, because he didn't know how "Jeena" had been programmed to respond to that eventuality.

He'd explain to the Count that he was grateful, and deeply honored, but that he had an aversion to pleasure androids (maybe he'd seen too many Gloriya movies?), and could they not reward him with a cheaper model instead, a straightforward service android for cooking and cleaning?

Then he had a slight change of heart. "Jeena" might not be human, but it was fabulously attractive, and he'd never have such an opportunity again. So why not take advantage of the android's manual services, at least? And he could *imagine* that it was the real Jeena…

CHAPTER THIRTEEN

AT THE ENQUIRY

Burk was an invited guest at the enquiry, not a witness. He would sit with the other members of the public, who almost without exception would also be invited guests or selected journalists, since this supposedly "public" enquiry was actually going to be very restricted.

His name would not be on a list of witnesses, so the Government might not have been forewarned about his appearance at the enquiry. Would they have double-checked the guest list? Their agents would probably have noticed his absence from his living unit, and they might have speculated that the thugs from Ideology had murdered him, but they would now be reassured to see him sitting among the "public." They knew about his friendship with Guardian Silvia—why shouldn't he be there as her guest?

And if they wanted to call him as a witness, theoretically they could. As could the Imperial Advisory Council, too. But the Count had instructed him that, if they wished him to testify, His Excellency, who would be presenting the case for the Council, would give him a prearranged signal and he should then "volunteer" to give evidence. That would seem less suspicious. In fact, anyone present at the enquiry could ask to be allowed to give evidence, at the discretion of the Chairperson. It was only an en-quiry, it wasn't a trial.

The Guardsman Stepharn had collected him from the guest living unit and driven him the two blocks to the enquiry. It was being held in a medium-sized public hall close to the Palace.

At the entrance they presented their invitations to the Ideology Guardians who were providing security, but there was no identity scan.

Stepharn explained: "Those Government technicians can manipulate the scanners. Who knows what they might do? So this is better!"

He was less pleased when they were body-searched, and he was asked to surrender his taser. They also found, and confiscated, a vicious-looking double-edged hunting knife.

"Shame on you, Guardian! Being a Guardsman doesn't give you the right to carry this sort of shit!"

They may have been on the same side, but Burk sensed that the Ideology Guardians rather resented the pampered, snobbish Imperial Guards. They were *men*, they had fancy uniforms and they were granted the status of Grade II Guardians automatically—they didn't have to earn it the hard way like everyone else.

Once inside the hall, Stepharn found a Guardsman colleague, Denyss, who was serving as a court usher, and asked him what exactly the fuck was going on?

"Is this *our* show or isn't it?"

It was indeed their show, his colleague explained, but the Chairperson was a ridiculous old pedant who thought there should be no weapons inside a courtroom. And in this case maybe he wasn't so stupid: it was going to be a showdown between the Government and the Council, and if any of the Guardians lost their cool and there was a taser shootout, wouldn't that give the Government an excuse to close down the whole event?

"He's our man alright—the Government arseholes forced him to retire, so he hates their guts—but he has to do it by the rules. Who's your little friend, by the way?" (Burk was by no means small, but Guardsmen were always enormous) "I smell AdPop. You shagging him, or what?"

Stepharn was not amused. Guardian Denyss dropped the banter and showed them to their seats. These were benches made of real wood, not the synthetic kind. Burk was delighted, and enjoyed tracing the knots and whorls in the wood with his fingers.

Everyone stood up when the Chairperson and his two assessors entered. Retired Judge Erivan was a crusty old character with a permanently miserable expression on his face, as though his piles were getting to him. Maybe they were?

Guardian Silvia hadn't changed in the least, and once the proceedings were under way she gave Burk a friendly little wave. This had the effect of briefly drawing everyone's attention to him. Heads craned round, and the Government attorney, Guardian Grade IV Ronold, fixed Burk with a grim "So the little shit has shown up after all!"-look.

Only the Count ignored him. As did the second judicial assessor, who seemed to be asleep most of the time (which might have been why they had chosen him).

The Count was invited to open on behalf of the Imperial Advisory Council. With great fluency, and a highly professional muiltimedia presentation, he accused the Government of manifold abuses of trust on Lemnos, including the large-scale destruction of *sqot*. His presentation was centered on the same forged documentation that Burk and Milliya had been fed by the wealthy settler Jonn.

Burk tried to remain expressionless, not giving away what he thought about the "evidence", and did his best to clear his mind of any thoughts about the matter, just in case the Government had smuggled a telepath into the hearing. But he was given a jolt when he heard the Count say that he reserved the right to call the AdPop John Burk as a witness, should His Honor the Chairperson wish for further corroboration of the Government's shocking behavior.

Next, the Count launched into an attack on the Government for secretly factory-farming *sqot* in Africa. He supported this with an even more impressive presentation of documentary evidence, which Burk guessed might well be genuine.

When the Count finally sat down, Judge Erivan pointed out that the time for the lunch recess was approaching. In the interests of fairness, however, the attorney for the Government should be allowed to make a brief initial response to the Council's accusations.

"'Brief' being the operative word, Guardian Ronold, because our lunch is waiting for us!"

And he looked at his former colleague from Justice as if he had about as much affection for him as he did for his hemorrhoids.

"Thank you, Your Honor, but with your permission the Government's arguments will be presented in full detail this afternoon. For the moment, suffice it for me to say that the documentation presented by my honorable colleague the Secretary to the Council is *fake*! Both sets of so-called evidence are malicious forgeries. We could even have proved this directly, if we had been able to call as a witness the former Guardian Milliya Jahangiri. Unfortunately she has disappeared. We have strong reason to believe that she was abducted by agents of the Imperial Advisory Council. She was probably tortured, to find out how much she knew, and may have been murdered. But our search for her will continue. We shall not give up."

Judge Erivan interrupted the attorney.

"By all means continue with the search, provided it is not allowed to keep us from our lunch!"

There was a titter of laughter, which clearly annoyed Guardian Ronold. He now slightly lost his cool.

"That is only *one* example of how the Council has attempted to muddy the waters and prevent its misdeeds from becoming public knowledge! Our investigators on Lemnos have been stymied at every turn by settlers in league with the Council. And the AdPop creature Burk, sitting there so shamelessly among the public, a loathsome pedophile by the way, has been *bought* by the Council, no doubt with sordid privileges, and the promise of the numerous charges against him being dropped! *His* testimony—should my honorable colleague the Secretary have the temerity to call him—is therefore utterly worthless!"

Burk felt his scalp tingling, and imagined that he had probably blushed bright red. He was angry, too: hadn't it been Guardian Sousanna who had promised him that the charges against him would be dropped?

Everyone was now looking at him again. Guardsman Stepharn nudged him jocularly in the ribs.

"How do you like being famous?" he muttered.

Burk didn't.

Judge Erivan now brought the morning session to a close, and the public filed out into the entrance hall, where a modest buffet lunch had been spread out on trestle tables. It was modest indeed, compared with what Burk had been served on the Imperial Viewing Platform. Most of it was still wrapped or packaged, and the brand name DELICIO was much in evidence. As if that wasn't enough to put Burk off his food, he had the distinct impression that the "loathsome pedophile" was being shunned. Even Guardsman Stepharn was noticeably keeping his distance.

Either a lot of people had suddenly turned up for the food (which was hard to believe!), or the afternoon session was going to be more crowded than the morning session had been. Among the new arrivals were Guardians Rebek'a and Sousanna and their entourages, including Guardian Julieta, traipsing behind her mistress, and Guardian Anfea, following hers. All of them had been disarmed and looked thoroughly bad-tempered.

Which was not surprising: Guardians didn't like being stripped of their tasers. Burk remembered an old joke from his schooldays: "A Guardian without her taser is like a fart without an arsehole!"

Guardian Rebek'a pretended to be interested in the food on the table in front of Burk, then "accidentally" knocked the plate out of his hand. As he knelt to retrieve the plate and the food items, the unwrapped ones at least, she leant forward and whispered, "Rot in hell, Burk. I would have had you dismembered—*slowly*. But the Count has a soft heart. So if you're called, just be a good boy and say your party piece as you've been told. And never cross my path again. That's all."

Then he was alone once more. For a few minutes, and without much enthusiasm, he unwrapped and ate some of the food. It was DELICIO muck, but superior "Guardian rations", so probably there wouldn't be any reprocessed human organic material in the ingredients.

His next visitor was Guardian Sousanna.

"Good to see you alive and well, Burk. I hear you spent the evening with Satan? Don't worry; I doubt whether you'll be called. They don't think they need you, and nor do we. Now eat up your food, and in five minutes go and empty your bladder. Don't go to the toilets in the cellar. Take the elevator and use the hygienic area for the physically challenged up on the next floor. Have a long, enjoyable piss!"

"But I don't need to go. And, anyway I'm not—"

"Just do it, Burk."

Burk was inclined not to. What if it were a trap? The Government was worried about his testimony. Everyone now knew he'd been "turned". Burk hadn't seen any physically challenged people at the hearing, so the up-stairs toilet would be empty and quiet...except for the killer who could be waiting for him there. And to make it look like a mugging, it wouldn't even be a taser; it'd be a wire noose, or a razor, smuggled in past the security.

On the other hand, he couldn't imagine Guardian Sousanna, his Pallas Athene, willingly being involved in such a vile, messy murder.

Still, she *was* a Guardian.

With a sinking heart and a heavy step, he made his way to the elevator and then to the hygienic area for the physically challenged. As expected, it was empty. He stood at one of the stalls and tried to do what Guardian Sousanna had told him to, but nothing came.

Where was the killer, then? This was the ideal moment for her to strike. And, sure enough, Burk heard a footfall, and sensed a movement behind him. Then another human body was pressed against him, and he felt breath on the back of his neck.

"Hello, Burk."

It was Milliya.

CHAPTER FOURTEEN

THE FOURTH FORCE

Burk gawped at her. His first thought was that she had been sent to kill him, but she was smiling very sweetly.

He had a million things to ask her, but nothing came out.

"Struck silent? Not a word to say? That's not very flattering. I'm supposed to be your lover…"

He pulled himself together. Where had she been? Why had she gone with the Ciaranites?

And: "It was no thanks to *you* that they didn't kill me!"

"I'm sorry, Burk, I've got a lot of explaining to do. I've been playing a rather complicated game."

"How does Guardian Sousanna know you're here? Have you changed sides? Did they rescue you? Are you working for *her* now?"

Milliya shook her head.

"No. I went to her this morning. I've told her where the communicator with the recordings is hidden, and her people are fetching it now."

"So you escaped from the Ciaranites?"

"No, they let me go." She saw his look of astonishment. "Yes, really! I persuaded them. They hate the Government, but do you think they want *the Council* to take over? You know, all that stuff about Africa is genuine—so the Government is doomed, this enquiry will make sure of that. But if the Council can be exposed as well… Then they won't be able to take over and rule by Imperial Rescript. There'll have to be elections, free ones, and perhaps even a moderate regime afterwards?"

"And then the Ciaranites will hand in their weapons."

"That'll never happen. They're fanatics. They're crazy. What they're doing is only tactical: to bring down the Government and shaft the Council at the same time. The war isn't over. It won't be till they've achieved their weird version of paradise, and that'll mean killing anyone who doesn't obey them. People like you and me."

She told Burk that the Government attorney was now evaluating the information on her communicator ("No lunch for *him*!") and would present it during the afternoon session. Then he would call upon her to testify. Burk's testimony wouldn't be needed.

Guardian Sousanna had got her into the building secretly. Milliya's life was obviously in danger, but all the Guardians had been disarmed. That wouldn't prevent them from trying to assassinate her, by some trick or other, but when the session started she'd slip into the hall with Burk and sit next to him. She didn't think they'd do it in public, what with everything at the enquiry being recorded.

"And once I've given my testimony—"

"—the cat is out of the bag!"

"I beg your pardon?"

"Never mind."

Milliya accompanied him back into the hall. At first no-one noticed her. Then there were whispers. People pointed her out to each other, and Burk saw Guardian Rebek'a, fortunately trapped on the far side of the crowded chamber, talking animatedly into her communicator. Where was Guardian Julieta, though?

The whispering stopped when Judge Erivan re-started the proceedings. What should have happened next is that Guardian Ronold would rise to his feet, ask for permission to begin, and then lay out the case for the Government.

It didn't happen that way, though. In fact, things started to unravel.

A member of the public interrupted the judge, demanding the right of a citizen (and high-ranking Guardian) to make an urgent contribution to the enquiry.

Judge Erivan looked distinctly irritated. But he was a known stickler for protocol, and so the man was invited to come forward to the witness stand to be sworn in. He looked vaguely familiar to Burk, who hadn't had many dealings with senior Guardians: this was not someone that he knew, though he was sure that he'd seen him before.

He was tall and slim, a man of distinguished bearing. In the witness stand, he asked to take the standard oath on the Honor and Manifest Destiny of Terra (rather than one of the dozens of oaths still tolerated in connection with cults and superstitions). He announced his name: he was Guardian Grade IV Mykel Angelos, Commander of the *Starstretcher*.

Commander Mykel explained who he was, and declared that it was his conscience that had prompted him to take this step. He was a spokesman for neither the Government nor the Imperial Advisory Council, although he had become aware of the illicit activities of both of them, most recently on a journey to Lemnos and back.

On the outward trip, the AdPop John Burk—Burk felt all eyes turned on him again—was detained under ridiculous, trumped-up charges by the Government agent Guardian Sousanna Alpheios. And he actually pointed an accusing finger at her! She blushed in embarrassment. To Burk's relief, all eyes now swiveled to stare at *her*.

On the return trip, the Commander had witnessed the peculiar and illegal behavior of another senior Guardian, Rebek'a Lascaris from Ideology.

"And there she is, still at large!" He pointed the accusing finger again. "Apparently no-one has followed up the Form 85a Complaint that I filed against her."

Once again the eyes swiveled. Guardian Rebek'a didn't blush, but stared back at him angrily.

"Yes, yes, Commander, this is all very interesting, and *colorful*. Does it justify your interrupting the hearing so dramatically, though? Do you have a point of major pertinance that you wish to make, or may I ask attorney Guardian Ronold to begin with his arguments on behalf of the Government? He *claims* to have an interesting new witness."

The Commander's eyes flashed.

"Yes, Your Honor, I *do* have a point of major pertinance to make."

The judge sighed, but asked him to continue.

For many years, he said, the Government had secretly been importing *sqot* into Terra. This was with the active cooperation of Fleet Commanders like himself. His colleagues had accepted large payments in return for their help in facilitating this criminal activity. At some point a colleague, knowing of his financial problems, had approached him and, to his eternal shame, he had agreed. He had only accepted such a payment once, but it was once too often. When he had finally learnt what the *sqot* was being used for, he knew that he had no option but to make a confession andf throw himself on the mercy of Terran justice.

"And for the moment, that is all I have to say."

Judge Erivan now looked uncommonly pleased with himself. There could be no doubt where his personal sympathies lay. The sudden appearance of Milliya as a witness for the Government must have annoyed him, Burk thought, but this had been trumped by the revelations they had just heard.

He asked the Commander to step down, and to hold himself at the further disposal of the enquiry. The decision whether to prosecute him, or to offer him immunity in return for his evidence, would be taken after the hearing had ended, and by the judge himself. The Minister of Justice could scarcely be expected to be impartial in the matter, could she?

The two attorneys both rose simultaneously to their feet to voice their respective requests or objections. The judge waved to them to be silent.

"In making this statement, Guardian Mykel is incriminating himself most substantially—and for that reason alone, his testimony to me seems wholly convincing. I shall have to consult with my assessors on this, but I can safely say that, whatever else this enquiry may recommend, it is likely to ask His Imperial Majesty to dissolve the present Government, pending legal investigations and preparations for new elections, with all necessary executive measures in the interim period to be announced by Imperial Rescript."

Guardian Ronold was outraged.

"Your Honor, I represent the legitimate elected Government of Terra—"

"Objection, Your Honor!" The Count was triumphant. "Can the word 'legitimate' be used to describe a body of ruthless women engaged in smuggling onto this planet in large quantities the most dangerous substance in the universe?"

Judge Erivan nodded in agreement, and that should have been that. But now the hearing took its second unexpected turn.

Guardian Silvia leant across to the judge and whispered something to him. He looked at her thoughtfully, and then consulted the second assessor, who was now fully awake and involved in the proceedings.

"It seems that we shall have a short interlude before continuing. My distinguished colleague Guardian Silvia has made a request that I can hardly refuse, especially as it concerns a general point of procedure rather than a strict point of law. We have been hearing about *sqot* at great length, but my two assessors have never actually *seen* it. Nor, I daresay, have many of you here assembled had that privilege either. I, on the other hand, have been fortunate, and by a happy coincidence it was thanks to *you*, Your Excellency, at a small reception that you hosted at the Imperial Palace on Terran Unity Day this year. So let some *sqot* be brought here for a viewing! Bring in two of those tables from the entrance hall, and someone fetch a couple of containers with *sqot*! Let us all take a good look at this remarkable substance! It will also give you two gentlemen a chance to calm down before we return to more serious matters."

Far from calming down, the Count protested.

"Your Honor, there is surely no need here for any light entertainment. It would detract from the seriousness of this enquiry, especially at a stage when devastating and convincing accusations have just been made against the Government. 'Convincing' was the word that you yourself used. We should press on—"

That was a mistake. The judge glowered at the Count.

"How this enquiry will be run is for *me* to decide! Do not presume upon our friendship, Your Excellency! My colleagues wish to see *sqot*, and *sqot* they will see! One of your Guardian staff shall accompany my ushers to the Palace to fetch it. I know that you have a small amount there still, for your own private purposes. I am better informed than you imagine, Your Excellency."

Burk and Milliya didn't dare to move while the viewing was being organized. If one of the Ideology Guardians could get close to them, Milliya could be dispatched, for example, by a sharp, carefully placed blow to a nerve behind the neck. Or by a pinprick of poison. In the excitement, who would notice? Luckily, the other invited guests sitting around them remained just where they were, though they were abuzz with anticipation. It wasn't every day that you got to see *sqot*.

Two tables were brought in, and placed in front of and parallel to the raised platform where the judge and his assessors were seated. Soon afterwards the ushers returned, carrying two large and very ornate containers, one of which was put on each table. At a sign from Judge Erivan, the ushers removed the lids and stepped back quickly.

"There we have it: *sqot*! My honorable colleagues will now view the substance, and afterwards the members of the public may come forward row by row to do the same."

The viewing was done in an orderly fashion. Nobody wanted to go too close to the stuff, or stand directly in front of it for too long. Guardsman Stepharn whispered loudly, "What's the big deal with this muck?" and someone behind them responded, "You get an orgasm when you eat it!"

After the last group had returned back to its row, the judge said, "Now that we all know what *sqot* looks like, we may continue!"

But before he could, Guardian Silvia leant across to him and whispered something to him again. He nodded.

"You Excellency," he said, beckoning the Count to come forward, "we require a small clarification from you."

"Your Honor?"

"Your Excellency, a moment ago you referred to *sqot* as the most dangerous substance in the universe. Well, now we've all seen it, and it's not pretty or cuddly—but *dangerous*? Please elucidate on that."

"Your Honor, *sqot* has qualities and characteristics that we don't fully understand—"

"Naturally. This is an alien life form, after all, and requires to be studied. Which is what scientists are for! And we can condone the importation of a small amount of *sqot* for those purposes; not the smuggling of large quantities, of course. But why is *sqot* dangerous?"

"It may mean us harm, Your Honor."

The Count was standing in front of the two tables, and between the open containers. As if responding to his words, *sqot* began to rise over the side of each container and spread itself on the surface of the table. It glowed luminous green.

There was a deathly hush in the hall, and then a man in the front row shouted out, "It's evil!"

"Keep calm!" The Count turned to the public. "Whatever you do, don't provoke it!"

"Everyone should remain seated. This is very interesting, but how does it consitute a threat? Your Excellency, I'll ask you again: what reason do you have for describing *sqot* as dangerous?"

For the first time, Guardian Silvia spoke openly, and without even asking permission.

"He knows, because he's a telepath! He can read its mind!"

The judge turned to her angrily.

"Colleague, that he is a mild telepath is well-known to me, but it is not a matter to be mentioned in public. Telepaths have duties and obligations, but they are also protected by law."

"If he *can* read its mind, his legal duty is surely to tell us, Your Honor?"

"In this enquiry, I alone am responsible for points of law! But what you say is correct." He turned again to the Count. "What is it thinking?"

The Count took a step backwards.

"I don't know, Your Honor. I just get brief intimations..."

"Then stand *closer* to it, man, don't step backwards! This enquiry will not proceed until you have shown a willingness to cooperate. And that is very much in your interests, is it not, Your Excellency? You are asking for the Government to be suspended, and I am prepared to make that recommendation. But first *this*, if you please! Nothing will come of nothing!"

Unwillingly, the Count stepped forward again. The tables were now completely covered in a thin layer of *sqot*, which glowed with a sinister light and was throbbing slightly.

He began to speak, yet nothing came out, just a gurgling sound. With his face turned away from them, the public couldn't see what was happening, but the judge and his assessors stared at him in horror and jumped out of their chairs, pressing their backs against the wall behind them.

People began leaving the hall.

Then the Count screamed, a monstrous cry of despair that was choked off suddenly as if a huge hand had grasped his throat. He staggered, and turned around. His face was red, but the rest of the front of his body was covered with *sqot*, which had reached his neck. Then it slid up across his face, transforming it into a mask. The mouth gulped and disappeared, the eyes were sucked into the skull, and then his head dissolved into a shapeless lump of throbbing organic matter.

Sqot was slowly spreading onto the walls to either side of the rostrum and behind it, and onto the ceiling above. Judge Erivan and the assessors had already slipped away through a side-door. People were charging towards the exit doors, knocking over the benches as they went.

Burk and Milliya were among the last to leave. Somehow it seemed unlikely that anyone would now try to kill Milliya. Events had overtaken that danger—a new chapter in the history of Terra had begun, perhaps the final chapter, and who it was that had previously cheated, lied or murdered no longer seemed to matter.

It was not the Government, the Imperial Advisory Council, or the Ciaranites who would determine the fate of the planet, but a fourth force. Humans had gone to Lemnos; now *sqot* had come to Terra.

They stepped outside, leaving behind them the greed, lying and horror inside the building. Milliya took his hand. It was probably dusk—who could tell? On Terra there was never much daylight. Even during the day, the dim lights of the city would be left on, to flicker through the permanent Terran smog.

Except that, astonishingly, it wasn't dark. Hand in hand, they stared in amazement. Westwards from the city, the impenetrable wall of smog had cleared, as though someone had battered a hole in it, and Helios sat, huge and round, on the distant horizon. When it sank below it, there would definitely be darkness.

Burk and Milliya turned to each other, and as they did so the star trembled, slipped, and flashed its light one last time across everything, like a sudden, blinding reflection off metal; or the signal of the coming end of a planet.

APPENDIX: TERRAN SOCIAL STRATA

H. I. M. the Seventeenth Emperor

Guardian V—Senior leadership
H. E. Count Stelios Dagon (Secretary to the the Imperial Advisory Council)

Guardian IV—Junior leadership
†G. Dr. Ciaran Burke
G. (retired) Erivan (Justice)
G. Mykel Angelos (Commander of the *Starstretcher*)
G. Ronold (Government attorney, Justice)
G. Sousanna Alpheios (temporarily promoted to Guardian IV rank, Crime and Security)

Guardian III—Officers
G. Rebek'a Lascaris (Senior Level, Ideology)
†G. Adriyan (Social and Recreational)
G. Selwin (Crime and Security)
G. (retired) Silvia

Guardian II—Non-commissioned officers
G. Denyss (Imperial Guardsman)
G. Jeine Jahangiri (Science, Milliya's sister)
G. Julieta (Ideology)
G. Sirina (Crime and Security, "Pigface")
G. Stepharn (Imperial Guardsman)

Guardian I—Rank and file
G. Anfea
G. Jeena (Trainee, "Miss Bee-sting")
†G. Jo-anna Corticelli
G. Milliya Jahangiri
G. "Mr. Sensitive"

Useful population (UsePop)—Made up of "breeders" (f) and their "consorts" (m)
Aylwin (settler on Lemnos)
Gloriya (settler on Lemnos)
Jonn (settler on Lemnos, Gloriya's husband)
Jolyon

Additional population (AdPop)—Made up of "ladies" (f) and "drones" (m)
John Burk
Jacoob (scribe)
Keyzer ("The Source", downtown dealer)
López (janitor)

Surplus population (SurPop)—Underclass, convicts, criminals, addicts, social undesirables
"Octopus"
"Boss Man"

ABOUT THE AUTHOR

Francis Jarman was born in Germany but brought up and educated in England. According to a dubious tradition, his mother's side of the family is descended from the Roman slave Androcles (of *Androcles and the Lion* fame). He is a playwright, a novelist, a specialist in cultural studies and intercultural communication, and a classical numismatist. On his travels he has met a goddess, witnessed the hold-up of a train by bandits, danced in public with eunuchs, stroked a lion, sat on a snake, encountered sacred rats—and been attacked by a pig, detained by an army patrol, and beaten up by the police. He now lives (quietly) in Berlin.